HERO OF
LESSER CAUSES

JULIE JOHNSTON

HERO OF
LESSER CAUSES

Lester Publishing Limited

Canadian Cataloguing in Publication Data

Johnston, Julie, 1941-
    Hero of lesser causes

ISBN 1-895555-22-1 (bound)   ISBN 1-895555-43-4 (pbk.)

I. Title.

PS8569.O56H4 1992   jC813'.54   C92-092041-7
PZ7.J65H4 1992

Lester Publishing Limited
56 The Esplanade
Toronto, Ontario
M5E 1A7

Printed and bound in Canada

  94 95 96 5 4 3

ACKNOWLEDGEMENTS

I wish to thank Doctors Don Clark and Tony Guzman for patiently answering my questions about polio, and Professor Michael Treadwell for his generous editorial assistance. Also, I am indebted to Kathy Lowinger, my editor, for her unflagging optimism during difficult times, and for her unerring sense of direction. I am grateful to Budge Wilson, whose encouragement came at the right time, and to Erica Perk, whose faith proved invaluable. I gratefully acknowledge the involvement of my sisters and the encouragement and forbearance of other friends through long lunches, miles of cycling, vintage tastings, cups of café au lait and hands of bridge.

For Mae Dulmage and in memory of Barney Dulmage;
for Basil;
and for Leslie, Lauren, Andrea and Melissa.

CHAPTER

1

It started off as a peaceful, plodding kind of summer, the summer of 1946. We didn't know that our lives would charge wildly out of control.

The war had been over for a year, although my brother, Patrick, and I were still taking part in it as much as possible. We had given up shooting each other, mainly because we were too old; I was twelve and Patrick was thirteen and a half that summer, and also because my mother didn't like to hear me going around ack-acking and ptchooing at Patrick. "Keely," she said, "girls don't do that." I didn't ever tell her this, but I used to think, what if I was in the war and they were coming right at me with guns and bombs and everything they could think of, I'd dig in my heels, grit my teeth and hold up the flat of my hand. I'd wither them. Floor them. You just have to think hard enough about something and you can do anything. Usually. Well, maybe not always.

Being too old to shoot each other didn't stop us from planting stink-bombs in each other's beds. Or ambushing each other. Once I leaped out from behind the garage with the garden hose aimed full blast. As it turned out, it was Mother's footsteps I heard on the cracked cement of our driveway, not Patrick's. She isn't what you'd call a good sport at times like that. Neither is our father. He's a judge and has a position to uphold. And so do all of you, he keeps telling us. He made this clear the day he heard that Patrick marched downtown with his hair plastered in a straight line over his left eye and a square, black moustache under his nose. I dared him to. Adolf Hitler spent next day cleaning the garage. He vowed to get me back.

By the middle of August it was so hot that even in the morning we stuck to the chairs in the kitchen. Patrick and I were sitting at the kitchen table after breakfast, trying to think of things to do if we could get off the chairs. Patrick was at loose ends because his friend Donald was away. I had my arms folded in front of me on the table and my head down resting (stuck, actually) on my arms. With one finger I nudged a sweating glass of milk, left over from breakfast, towards the edge of the table. It was one of those finish-your-milk-and-then-you-can-leave-the-table situations. I tapped and prodded until it was at the brink. Patrick had a pencil and paper and was doodling as he usually did, drawing horses' heads. He was also watching what I was doing, not taking his eye off the glass. I pushed it a little farther until it hung over the edge. Our eyes met now. We didn't say anything. We didn't have to. Patrick looked at the glass on the verge of falling off the table; he looked at my finger just touching the base of the glass. His eyes flashed a dare and mine answered.

"Keely!"

We hadn't noticed our mother come into the kitchen. The glass toppled over. Patrick's hand shot out and caught it, but the milk went flying all over the floor.

"Outside!" she ordered. We peeled ourselves off the chairs and headed for the door.

"I'll clean it up," I offered, standing holding the door open, letting flies in. I pushed my hair back out of my eyes so she could see I was sorry.

"It's easier to do it myself," she said, in that last-straw tone she gets sometimes.

Outside, the heat was so heavy it was like trying to walk through neck-high bathwater. Patrick said, "I bet you'd be afraid to walk that plank over the falls in Barnet Park."

"Bet I wouldn't." I was lying and Patrick knew it.

"Prove it," he said.

We walked through my friend Ginny's backyard, taking a shortcut to the park at the south end of town. I hollered for Ginny on our way through but she wasn't around. She could have been anywhere, and usually was. Ginny gets around. Mrs. Dickson, Ginny's mother, claims that Ginny has an independent streak which she finds most unbecoming. I think it's just fine.

In the park we climbed over a fence with a sign warning people to keep out of that area. I looked at the narrow plank that spanned two newly built bridge abutments, mentally trying to measure its width. The plank didn't look much wider than a tightrope. Water cascaded over a falls under the plank, making me light-headed. The water swirled over jagged rocks and rushed madly to join the main body of the river. Patrick stood on the board, not expecting me to follow, not even looking back. I took a deep breath, raked back my hair with a sweaty hand and said, "Okay, out of my way." I brushed past him, sliding one foot ahead of the other. I inched my way towards the middle, mumbling to myself, "Don't be stupid. Don't look down. Don't look down."

I looked down.

"Stupid!" I said out loud. I couldn't move. I tried praying but got stuck after "Our Father". Panic had me by the throat. I got down on all fours and crept, studying the board, memorizing it. This kept me crawling. I was getting slivers in my knees, but getting closer to the end of the plank all the same. "Thy kingdom come," I breathed finally, as I reached the other side and scrambled onto firm, grassy ground. I ducked under a chain with a sign similar to the one on the other side, DANGER KEEP OUT, and looked back at Patrick. He was shuffling along, sliding one foot, then the other, his arms outstretched for balance.

"Hey, you guys!" The voice was Ginny's. Patrick was halfway along the plank when she appeared on the shore on my side of the falls. He faltered, tipping backward, then forward, making circles in the air with his arms. Ginny and I sucked in air. Patrick caught his balance. Without taking his eyes off Ginny, he straightened his shoulders, his arms graceful as a dancer's, and — placing one foot in front of the other — increased his speed until, with a flying leap, he cleared the chain with the danger sign. Superman had landed. That's what it looked like, anyway.

"Holy!" Ginny said, her eyes all round and admiring. My heart had stopped for a moment but it started up again.

"You're such a show-off, Patrick," was all I said.

He put his hands in his pockets and strolled away whistling.

Ginny looked as if she were melting away. She had a thing about Patrick. I don't know why. ~~He was stubborn, the worst~~; he insisted he was right even when he was wrong. He wasn't often wrong, I had to admit. For a boy he was very intelligent. Talented, too, according to his teachers. He could draw and paint pictures better than anyone else in town, not that I cared. I had a talent or two of my own. Probably. Anyway, Patrick Connor was considered a regular Vincent van Gogh. With two ears. Everyone in town said so.

I flipped over into half a cartwheel and called Ginny. "Look at how far I can walk on my hands, Ginny. Hey, look. Patrick can't go half this far." But Ginny was still watching Patrick swagger along ahead of us.

What I like about Ginny is that independent streak her mother finds so unbecoming. She doesn't think about things; she does them. Like tobogganing off Old Man

Harkin's garage roof last winter. She didn't think about whether he'd be mad and chase her with part of an old eavestrough. She's a good runner. What I don't like about Ginny is the way she makes me feel invisible whenever Patrick is around. I'd like to put a question to her sometime. I'd say: If Patrick and I were in front of a firing squad and you had the power to save only one of us, who would you save? I know I'll never ask her that, because I'd probably be crushed by her answer.

I was right side up again. Ginny and I scuffed along shoulder to shoulder, Ginny smiling, probably thinking about Patrick and herself. I wasn't smiling, but I was thinking about Patrick and *my*self. And life.

I said, "I know why Patrick sets up dares. He likes to prove he's a winner. I guess I only do it to keep up to him. Know what I mean, Ginny?"

"No," said Ginny. She was still gazing at Patrick's back, which was getting farther and farther ahead of us.

"I mean, sometimes I think I'm only here because Patrick's here, that maybe without him I'm not even a person. Know what I mean?"

Ginny shook her head. "No," she said. Patrick turned the corner and was out of sight now.

"Look at it this way. I feel that if Patrick disappeared, I'd disappear too. Now do you know what I mean?" I looked hopefully at her, coming around to stand right in front of her.

"Keely," she said, "sometimes you're such a bore." That was Ginny's word that summer, the summer of 1946.

So maybe I am a bore. At least she didn't say I was a screwball. Often people did.

Ginny came over after lunch to swelter with me. We sat on our back stoop and wondered if we were too old to run through the sprinkler.

"We *could* go to the swimming pool," I suggested.

"Too boring," Ginny replied. "Anyway, I'm not allowed. Germs, you know."

"Patrick's going."

"We-e-ell...."

"We're not allowed either, but Patrick always goes."

"What about the germs?"

"You don't get germs; you get polio or something. But that's only in cities."

"What a bore."

Patrick swung into sight just then, his towel stuffed into his shirt. "Hurry up if you're coming," he said to me. "Mother's gone out so now's our chance." He flashed Ginny a challenge. "Coming?"

"Of course," she said, falling into step beside him.

"What a bore," I murmured, but nobody heard me. I walked along with my hair in my eyes.

Ginny and I were not invaded by germs. We didn't even catch summer colds after all our cannonballs and bellyflops with the other kids in Channing's public swimming pool. All three of us returned to our place and sprayed each other with the hose to explain our wet hair. We lounged lazily on the grass under a maple in our front yard. It was too hot, even, to play cards.

I said, "You can think yourself into being cool, you know."

Patrick was pulling up grass blade by blade and throwing it at Ginny. He stopped long enough to argue with me. "No you can't. You can't think up a drop in temperature."

"You can do anything if you think hard enough about it," I insisted.

"You can't fly."

That nearly stopped me. "Riding a fast horse would be like flying."

"Some people can't even draw a horse, let alone ride."

"Here we go again," said Ginny. She threw grass back at Patrick, but he didn't notice.

"Let's see you think your way into drawing a recognizable horse, Keel." Another challenge. Patrick had a way of smiling knowingly and looking sideways at Ginny which infuriated me. If Ginny grinned back at him, I'd kill her. There are times when girls ought to stick together. Boys do automatically.

Ginny lay back in the grass with her arm over her eyes, ignoring both of us.

"I'm not talking about drawing," I said, "I'm talking about riding. Drawing's too simple."

"Simple for me, anyway." Patrick was right, of course. He just had to pick up a pencil to produce a sleek racehorse. He could spend a whole rainy day drawing horses running or jumping fences or standing still. I always wanted him to give his horses riders but he never would. Even though I believed I could do anything if I thought about it hard enough, I knew from experience that whenever I tried to draw a horse it turned out looking like a potato on toothpicks. Even after deep thought.

"Who'd want to sit around drawing horses when you could easily ride one?" I was kneeling in front of Patrick now, so that I could stare him right in the face. This was an ongoing challenge. So far nothing had come of it.

"You can't ride a horse if you haven't got a horse." His standard reply.

"I've heard all this before," Ginny sighed. She sounded as though she might fall asleep.

I continued my dare. "We could sneak into Laurence Saunders' field and ride Lightning."

Patrick groaned and leaned back against the tree trunk, flicking grass at me now. "Lightning only exists in your one-track mind, Keely. Count 'em. There's fat Lola." He held up a finger. "And there's dumb Bill." He held up another finger. "Calling Lola 'Lightning' won't turn the old nag into a racehorse. Face it. And anyway, you can't ride either horse without permission."

"Who'd know?"

"If you fell off and broke something, everybody within ten miles would know."

I sat back and checked my bare knees for grass stains. I didn't want to look right at him. "You're scared, aren't you?"

Patrick snorted. "Don't be ridiculous. Look, let's just drop it, okay? It's too hot."

Only one knee was grass-stained so I rubbed grass into the other one. Ginny told us we were both being bores.

The reason we were on more or less intimate terms with horses was because of where we lived, at the extreme west end of Channing. Channing is a small town in the lower Ottawa Valley. I should explain about the Ottawa Valley. It's a river valley, not a mountain valley. But there's more to it than geography. My father says it's more a state of mind than a place. It has a personality.

To the east and across the street from us were houses; beyond our place to the west was countryside — farmland and bush. Our backyard looked out on our neighbour Laurence Saunders' small farm, separated from our garden by a rail fence. Beyond the fence, pastureland sloped gently uphill to where the love of my life, Lola/Lightning, liked to graze on the dry August grass or shelter under a clump of birches. Often, I leaned on the fence and watched the horse take long draughts from the creek that meandered through Laurence Saunders' property, trickled into a culvert under Fairly Street, our street, and widened into a shallow, nearly stagnant pool in the woods nearby. The pool was known locally as Bloodsucker Pond. You'd have to be out of your mind to put a bare limb into Bloodsucker Pond, for obvious reasons.

If you didn't count the pond, it was a fine part of town to live in. Maybe it was because our father was a County Court judge that he seemed to weigh things one against the other, even when he wasn't in court. Living on the edge of town was as good as living in the country, he was fond of saying. "We have the best of both worlds. Six blocks from our front door takes us to the centre of town [the court-house where Father spent much of his time was in the centre of town], and behind us, from our back door, we can breathe in the pure country air." Our mother shook her head sometimes. Breathing in the country air had its drawbacks, especially when Laurence Saunders got busy with the manure-spreader. He was a part-time farmer only, but that part was just too much as far as Mother was concerned.

"You watch," she had often said. "When the war ends, this street will see houses spring up like mushrooms." The war had ended, but the street remained much the same. There were rumblings around town, however, my father admitted — about development, about progress, about Laurence Saunders wanting to get ahead in the world. The other part of Laurence's job was hitching his old horse, Bill, to the breadwagon and plodding up and down the streets of Channing delivering bread to the customers of Quinlan's Bakery.

Ginny came to life, probably because Patrick and I had finally stopped arguing. We were just foot-fighting now, pressing the soles of our feet together trying to dislocate each other's ankles. Ginny sat up so we stopped. "What's so big about horses, anyway?" she wanted to know. She had asked the question before, but we had never got round to giving her a straight answer, at least not one that she said made sense. One thing about Ginny, she never gives up. Here she was, asking the question again.

"They're...noble animals," I said, not very helpfully.

I'll admit right here that my passion is horses. I read books about horses; I went to Saturday matinée cowboy movies just to admire the horses. Ginny usually went along too, but she went to admire the cowboys. The thing is, I think I've always had this vision of myself charging through a sort of mist on a silver-white stallion, up and down, say, the Ottawa Valley — probably the only place where this could happen — fixing things, making everything all better, riding like crazy over the vile and the petty to rescue the faint-hearted, while along the roadside crowds cheer and roar, "Keely the Connor rides again!" This is not something I talk about.

Ginny was trying to get Patrick to tell her what was so big about horses.

"Horses," he said, "are symbolic." Symbolic was Patrick's word that summer. I laid claim to it too.

"What does that mean?" Ginny was beginning to sound bored.

"Too hard to explain if you don't know." Patrick looked over at me; I looked back at him with just a tiny movement of my head. He blinked. Sometimes we were like Siamese twins joined at the mind, catching each other's thoughts through a nod or a glance. We had decided to enlighten Ginny. I ploughed back my hair, yanking it a bit to help me think clearly. I said, finally, "Heroes ride horses. That's what's so big about them."

Ginny didn't say anything. She looked into my eyes, then Patrick's, as if we were kidding or something. She must have seen that we were serious. Her face was blank, then a little disappointed. "I don't get it."

Ginny's mother called her, then, from the Dicksons' front porch across the street and down a bit. When Mrs. Dickson bellows, you don't hang around. Ginny jumped up. We looked at her mother with her hands on her hips, her elbows pointing east and west. "Oh-oh," Ginny said through her teeth. "I'm in trouble."

"What for?"

"Not sure. Can't remember." She set off at a trot.

Patrick called, "See you later."

She looked back, sliced her fingers across her throat and

wobbled her head. "Help!" she mouthed.

Patrick and I were still sitting on the grass, leaning on our hands, tanned skinny legs stretched out in front, foot to foot. We looked at each other and laughed because Ginny's not the type to need help. Neither were we.

Or so I thought.

2

The heat wave continued for more than a week. Mother kept the windows and drapes closed for most of the day to lock out the heat, but it managed to sneak in anyway. Father bought a fan. Patrick and I and even Mother lay on the living-room floor through the heat of the afternoon with the fan blowing hot air over us. But at least it was moving hot air.

I phoned Ginny a couple of times but she could never come over. She was serving time for several crimes. "What did you do?" I asked her.

"Don't ask," she sighed. She promised to phone when she was granted parole.

Every day we listened to the radio soap operas: "Life Can Be Beautiful," "Ma Perkins," "Pepper Young's Family" reached us at top volume over the roar of the fan.

It took a thunderstorm to finally clear the air. I went outside and stood in the middle of it with my head tilted back and my mouth open, trying to drink the new coolness. I yelled at Patrick to come out, but he didn't answer.

The rain ended and almost immediately the sun came out, making the road and even the trees look newly polished. Patrick needed an adventure to wake him up. He had become lazy, listless, even taking the heat into consideration. I went in to torment him. He was lying on the couch listening to "Road of Life." I turned the radio off but he didn't seem to notice. The worst dare in the world took shape in my head. He would have to take it or be forever humiliated. I got his attention. "I dare you," I said slowly, dramatically, "to wade into THE POND and stay there for three minutes."

"What pond?" He knew all right. His eyes gave him away.

"Bloodsucker, of course. Three minutes by the clock."

He looked pale, but he clenched his teeth and got up off the couch. We walked west down the road, not saying much. I knew I'd have to wade in too, if he actually did it. I was hoping he'd trip and break a leg so we could get out of this.

Ooze squished between our toes and slithery things flicked around our ankles and calves as we stood, knee-deep, in murky pond water. Patrick sucked in his cheeks and stared at his watch. I held my breath, or tried to, and counted, starting at a thousand. "Done!" Patrick said. It seemed like a day and a half later. We got out fast. When I saw six black, slimy bloodsucking leeches clinging lovingly to my feet and ankles, I heaved up my lunch. Tears came into my eyes, although I wasn't really crying. Vomiting does that to you. Patrick picked the leeches off his legs and flung them away quickly. I was breathing fast, thinking I might throw up again.

"I might as well take those off for you. I'm pretty well used to it now." He tried to make his voice sound rough but it came out sounding kind.

I said, "Sure," in as offhand a way as I could manage. I let my bangs fall forward so he couldn't see my watery eyes.

We shambled along the side of the road away from the pond. Patrick seemed drained of energy and I was still a bit queasy. As we approached his farm, Laurence himself came along the street, driving the breadwagon. He owned the wagon and he owned the horse. Rumour had it that he'd like to own the bakery too, if he could ever afford it.

My stomach settled immediately. "I'm going to ask him," I said. I moved a little ahead of Patrick.

"No you're not." Patrick grabbed the neck of my jersey and yanked me back but I wriggled free. I ran ahead to confront Laurence as the horse-drawn vehicle turned in at his lane.

"Nice horse," I said, nodding and pulling on my chin a bit. I wanted to look like an expert; I didn't want him to think this was just idle conversation.

"Eh?" He pulled back on the reins and the blinkered animal brought the breadwagon to a halt.

"That one up there." I pointed towards the high pasture, to his other horse.

"Not everybody's cup o' tea," he said.

"Wouldn't mind riding it."

"What? That!" Laurence scowled up at the mare sheltering in its arbour and looked dubiously back at me, sizing me up. "That's no merry-go-round horse, you know."

"Don't worry about me," I replied. "I've read books about how to ride a horse so I pretty well know everything." I glanced back at Patrick. He was just standing where I'd escaped his grasp, rubbing the side of his neck and blinking in the sunlight. He hadn't read anything about horses. The only thing he knew was how to *draw* a horse.

Laurence said he supposed I could give it a whirl. He patted the seat beside him. "Climb aboard." He motioned to Patrick to come along too. Patrick drifted towards us like a sleepwalker. I yelled at him and he came to long enough to get in.

The breadwagon, painted red with Quinlan's Bakery printed on both sides, had a bench seat in front and an overhang to protect the driver from the weather. The rest was a huge box which opened at the back to reveal trays like shelves for the loaves of bread. We joggled along as Bill clopped up the lane towards the driveshed. Laurence tied his feedbag on and unhitched him, and Bill munched and snorted and flicked his tail as if he was having the time of his life. Laurence went up into the loft then and brought down a cavalry saddle. He blew off the dust. "My uncle was the last to use this — thirty years ago in what they called the Great War."

I offered to carry the saddle. I felt so important I think I could have carried the horse too. Laurence handed Patrick the bridle and reins.

"Leave that stuff on the fence in the paddock near the barn and meet me in the high pasture," he said. "I have to get a line and some bait."

Puzzled, we watched him as he limped towards the house. He'd come out of the war with a game leg. "What does he mean, I wonder?" asked Patrick.

"It's just a horsey expression," I said knowledgeably. I'd look it up when I got home.

"Sounds more like a fishy expression to me."

"What would you know?"

Laurence, Patrick and I, armed with only a short rope and a tin cup filled with dry oatmeal cereal, made our way through the damp pasture towards the clump of trees where Lola stood sheltering from the recent rain.

"Let me know when the action starts," Patrick said. He climbed a pile of stones probably plucked from the field generations ago, and became a spectator. I peered at him from under a heavy brow. If this was a case of cold feet, it wasn't like Patrick to show it. I didn't comment.

"Come on, Lola, come on, girl," called Laurence. "Never was much use on the bread route, this one. Can't depend on her."

I couldn't call the horse of my dreams *Lola*. Automatically, I changed it to Lightning. "Here, Lightning," I called. "Come on, boy."

Lightning or Lola ignored both names. "She's a little deaf," said Laurence.

Walking towards my valiant steed, I don't recall my feet even touching the ground. I saw the horse's coat, faintly wet, glistening nut-brown in the afternoon sun filtering through the trees. Lola noticed our approach, twitched her tail and moved a little farther away, towards a grassy knoll. If the horse ambled on legs as thick as fenceposts, her neck bent as if the effort of holding up her head were too much, I didn't notice.

"What a noble head!" I exclaimed. In books, horses' heads are usually described as noble. "How many hands high is he?" I asked Laurence.

"Oh, she's big enough," he replied.

"Would you think eighteen?"

"Easily," said Laurence, "and about the same in width."

I took the rope and walked towards the horse. The horse waited until I was almost within touching distance before moving away. Again I approached; again the horse placed herself just out of reach. "Talk to her," called Laurence. He lit his pipe, pushed back his tweed cap and sat beside Patrick on the pile of heaped-up stones.

I talked, flattered, scolded, pleaded, to deaf ears. "High-spirited, isn't he." I was trying not to sound impatient.

"Stubborn, too," Laurence said. "Try and catch her with a bit of oatmeal. She loves it. Thinks it's a chocolate bar."

I took the tin cup and walked quietly up to the horse, holding the cup in front of me. Lightning/Lola looked interested. She stretched her neck towards the cup. She moved a little closer. Mesmerized, I stood still. The horse took another ponderous step forward, stuck its big, blunt nose into the cup and knocked it out of my hand. It fell to the ground with a clatter. Like a bolt of lightning, Lola took off for her tree shelter.

"Did you see that?" I shouted. "Did you see him run? Boy, can that horse ever move! He's obviously a winner."

"She's a real winner, all right," sighed Laurence. He

scooped up the spilled cereal into his hand, walked over to Lola, stuck a flattened palm under her nose and grabbed her halter as she began to snuffle and nuzzle up the flaky oatmeal. He led the horse over to the fence, from which I clambered onto her broad, bare back. Then he led Lola to the paddock where the saddle awaited. Patrick dragged along behind us. High above the ground I let my body sway and tilt with the three-dimensional movements of the horse.

"Now I know how a hero feels," I called back to Patrick. I don't think he heard me.

"Slide off and we'll saddle up," said Laurence. "Grab her halter, Keely, and hold her head." Lightning gave another example of his high spirits. Lola merely demonstrated that she wanted nothing to do with a saddle — she moved her hindquarters out of reach and snorted in my face. "Atta girl," said Laurence. "Easy now, easy." He tried again to place the saddle on Lola's back. Again she moved away.

"Tricky," I said.

"Only one thing you gotta remember." Laurence took off his cap. He was perspiring now. "You gotta let her know who's boss."

He tucked the stirrups up out of the way and made another lunge with the saddle. This time, when Lola moved, he was one step ahead of her. He slapped the saddle on just before she lurched into the rail fence.

"Help!" I was pinned against the fence by the horse's thick body. "Ouch!" Lola moved forward to stand chummily on my foot. I was beginning to have a fairly clear idea who was boss.

Finally Laurence gave the go-ahead. Waving away his offer of assistance, I climbed up and got a leg over the saddle. Laurence led us into the adjacent field. "Patrick!" I called. "There's nothing to it. You can be next." Patrick didn't answer. He sagged against the fence. As Laurence led Lola around in a wide circle, I straightened my back and held my wrists and elbows just so, like the pictures in my books, posing as a hero on a silver stallion.

It didn't matter that Laurence was a patient teacher or that I was an eager student. Lola had her own interests at heart, showing us who was boss. Laurence had to drag all fifteen hundred pounds of her down one side of the field. She ambled across the end, munching muddy bits of grass and weeds, and then at the corner, without batting an eye, she tore away towards the stable beyond the fence, dragging a gimpy-legged Laurence and me, bug-eyed and lopsided. The first few times this happened I nearly fell off. Then I found a way of pressing down hard in the stirrups and getting almost a scissors-lock on Lola's fat sides with my legs. By the time the next run rolled around, Laurence looked as though he might have a heart attack on the spot. I said, "Let go, Laurence. I'll be all right."

"Tighten the reins and pull b...." It was too late. Lightning was halfway up the field. Hanging on for dear life, I laughed like a lunatic. At the upper end of the field I had to get off to tempt Lola back on track with handfuls of grass. I glanced back at Patrick. That pinched look he had wasn't fear. It was something else. Something unsettling.

I turned my attention to the horse again, giving her one last offering of greenery before attempting to get my foot in the stirrup. Lola stretched her flabby lips around the bit to take the grass and for one brief moment I saw her flash a bossy little grin. I should have guessed she had a plan up her so-called sleeve. Laurence held her while I swung up into the saddle. I took up the reins and Laurence stepped away. Lola plodded across the field to the corner, where she must have been hit by black magic, because it was Lightning who blazed up and away towards the stable. This time she didn't slow down as she approached the fence.

"Ohmygosh!" I yelled. "He's going to jump!"

Laurence yelled something too, and started running up

the field. Patrick, wide-eyed, moved away from the fence. Lola, in full command now, stopped just short of the fence, and I was the one who nearly made the jump — right over her head. Grabbing the underside of her thick neck, I managed to slide under her, letting go finally to fall the short distance to the ground. As I lay under the horse, I was vaguely aware of a hoof pawing the ground close to my head. I tilted my head and had an upside-down view of Patrick moving, stumbling towards me. He got over the fence and snatched the horse's bridle with both hands, trying to push the stubborn animal back. The horse's head moved up and down with the power of a steam piston, her front hoofs dancing hard on the ground close to my ears. Patrick leaned all his weight against the horse's head, forcing her nose down. She backed up at last, her head moving from side to side, and I wriggled out of the way.

Patrick lost his footing then. He collapsed almost on top of me, gasping, choking, sobbing. I sat up, not believing this. My brother was crying! "It's all right," I said. "Patrick, I'm all right!" He cried and he kept on crying. "Patrick, you saved my life!" I scrambled to him and cradled his head on my lap. He winced in pain. He looked up at me with something in his eyes I'd never seen there before. He looked defeated.

"I think I'm sick," he said. His voice was hollow.

Channing closed its public swimming pool when it was learned that Patrick Connor had come down with a severe case of polio. Everyone in town said he would die.

3

But Patrick didn't die. He became paralysed.

I know, now, what being heartbroken is like. You feel as though you have an aching hole deep inside that nothing will ever soothe and nothing will ever fill. I couldn't tell anyone that, not even Ginny. I mean, what could other people say? They would say, oh, and look down at their feet. When the ache was really bad that fall, with Patrick away in the city in a hospital the size of Buckingham Palace, I used to skip school at recess and say I was sick. I *was* sick.

I couldn't see the point of school. Two pints one quart. Four pecks one bushel. Did they think I cared? I used to take a zigzag route, so no one could tail me, down to Barnet Park and lean over the railing of the bridge (they were afraid kids might try to walk the plank over the falls so they put in a bridge!) and watch the water tumble over the rocks and flow away. Beyond the rocks all you could see was the flat, grey river.

But they caught up with me. At least Father did. I suppose Mr. Leach, our teacher, mentioned something about me saying I was feeling sick all the time. Father said, "Getting poor marks in school isn't going to help Patrick get better." I thought about that. The way he said it, it sounded as though getting good marks *would*. I asked him and then wished I hadn't. He shook his head slowly in that

you-disappoint-me way he has and let out a deep sigh. I
made myself stop feeling sick at recess. I forced myself to
sit through Jock Cartier and Samuel D. Champlain explor-
ing around in the woods discovering lakes and countries
and furry animals. I still went down to the park, but after
four. Some days it was cold enough to see your breath.
Thanksgiving came. I didn't feel particularly thankful, but
Father said, "At least Patrick can breathe without needing
an iron lung. Thank Heaven for that." I saw pictures in the
paper, sometimes, of kids with polio, with their heads
sticking out of a huge metal oil-drum sort of thing. It was
something I didn't want to think about.

In the park I watched the leaves change from yellow and
red to a withered brown. I watched them drift from the trees
into the water below the bridge and get carried away by the
river. Some sank to the bottom and stayed there.

Ginny came with me sometimes, but usually she had to
practise the piano. Mrs. Dickson was using the Royal
Conservatory of Music to curb Ginny's independent streak.
By Remembrance Day the leaves had pretty well all flut-
tered down and it was snow that fell and disappeared, flake
after flake, into the river.

The weekend before Patrick's birthday, we went to visit
him and to take him presents. Mother had made him a plaid
bathrobe. "Thanks," he said without smiling. I thought
about the weeks she had spent on it, trying to match one
piece with the next so the plaid wouldn't jump around,
about the groans of frustration from her little sewing room,

"I hope it fits," Mother said.

Patrick didn't say anything. Father gave him a globe to
put on his desk. At first his eyes seemed to brighten, but

almost immediately they dimmed over. "Great," he said in a flat voice.

Quickly, I unwrapped the present I had for him. A razor and two blades. For the first time since his illness, his face showed an expression. He looked truly amazed. Or maybe it was more like shocked. Mother and Father both bent over to stare at his chin and his cheeks.

"Well." Father cleared his throat. "I don't think he'll wear it out before Christmas."

"So what?" I said. "It's having it that counts." I almost thought Patrick was going to laugh. But he didn't. He stared at the ceiling

As it got closer to Christmas, with no sign of Patrick being well enough to come home, I took to climbing the fence at the back of our garden into Laurence Saunders' pasture. Sometimes Lola braved the pinprick whirl of snow in the thick winter coat she had grown. If I took her an apple left over from the fall (we had more than usual without Patrick there to eat them) she'd let me stroke her neck. If I forgot the apple she'd clump off to the stable with all the charm of a woolly mammoth. I didn't usually bother going after her. I stood on the brow of the high pasture with my feet freezing inside my galoshes; I didn't care all that much. My hands were chapped raw from forgetting to wear my mitts, but I stuck them into the pockets of my parka and tried to think myself into becoming a cylinder of ice. It didn't work. It was almost dark by a quarter to five, when my mother usually called me to come in and get ready for dinner. I hated being in the house as much as I hated being in school, with no Patrick sitting across the dinner table and making me laugh when I drank my milk so that it came out my nose.

Early in the new year, it snowed non-stop for three days. When the sky cleared and the sun showed its face, the world looked like a fresh page. The snow was blindingly white. Walking home from school at noon hour, Ginny and I took turns walking with our eyes closed and leading each other. When I got inside I could barely make out Mother standing in the comparative darkness of the kitchen. Before I even had my coat unbuttoned, she told me that Patrick would be home by the end of February. I leaped around and cheered and carried on but she just stood there. She didn't even comment on the puddles of melted snow my galoshes had made. Toe against heel, I squeaked out of them. My eyes were adjusting to the indoor light. I watched Mother start to sit at the table and hesitate, start to move towards the stove and stop. She reminded me of someone lost.

I said, "I didn't know Patrick would get better all of a sudden like that."

"He didn't," she said.

I put my mitts on the kitchen radiator. "But. . . ."

"He's coming home because the doctors and physiotherapists can't do any more for him. They've done all they can."

"So? At least he's coming home. He might have to stay in bed a lot, but he could get up once in a while and walk around his room and then go back to bed." I took the lid off the pot on the stove and saw that it was creamed peas to put on toast — not everybody's favourite, maybe, but it was mine. My mother had made it specially.

"Keely. . . ." Mother's voice was as small as a child's. "He hasn't changed. He's the same."

I looked at her. Her eyes were wide and a bit red. I had seen Patrick at Christmas when we went to visit him in the huge hospital. I knew what she meant by "the same". He couldn't move. He could barely lift a finger. He couldn't turn over in bed; he couldn't sit up or feed himself or even hold a book. He could breathe and that was about all. He could talk, but usually he wouldn't. Mother had been crying and now I started. After I blew my nose I said, "But I thought he'd get better."

Mother went on in that uncertain voice. "His doctor said that if he made any progress it would be in the next few months. This is the telling year, he said. It's up to Patrick now."

My mother stood in front of the toaster, holding two slices of bread as if she didn't know what to do next. I flapped the sides of the toaster open for her and said, "If it's up to Patrick, then he'll be just flying around here like nobody's business." The element in the centre of the toaster glowed red. She laid the bread on the toaster sides and I flipped them closed. She didn't say anything. We watched the heat shimmer as the bread got toasty on the side next to the coil. I let the sides down again to turn the toast and closed them to brown the other side. It was something to do.

"The doctor says his disease seems to have defeated him; he has no desire to fight." Mother's voice quavered. "And if he doesn't fight, if he doesn't use his muscles, they'll waste away to almost nothing. He won't be able to use them even if he wants to."

"Patrick will get his fight back. I *know* him. He likes to win. He *loves* to win."

"The doctor said that at home he might find a reason to use what little muscle-power remains." We stood looking at each other. I guess we were both remembering what he had been like in the hospital. The toast was beginning to burn but neither of us rushed to save it.

During the interval before Patrick's return, January tried to wear us down, giving us only eight or nine hours of daylight each day. Most of that was spent in school, which added up to no daylight for me. There were things going on, skating on the school rink, the show Saturday afternoon, but nothing mattered except crossing off days on our new 1947 calendar. We had a thaw and then a twenty-below freeze-up. Lola was pretty content to stay in the stable now, and so was Bill when he wasn't pulling the breadsleigh — Laurence had made the change by replacing the wagon wheels with runners.

I went over to talk to the horses once or twice after school, muffled to the eyes with a scarf. Laurence was never around but I didn't think he'd mind. Walking across the pasture's snowdrifts to the stable was like using a rubber crutch. The crusty, glazed snow would support me for five steps and then one foot would sink in up to my knee. I'd drag it out and then the other one would sink in. I could have gone around by the road, but somehow I liked the struggle. Anyway, it took longer and gave me time to think about things, about Patrick and me and the way we used to dare each other to the limit. I tried to remember every event in our lives from the beginning of time, our time, right up until the summer just past.

I told a lot of this to the horses. They didn't say anything back, which was comforting. They just stood around smelling like summer gone overripe. I didn't mind. I liked to take off my mitts and rub their thick coats with my hands so I could take the smell home with me. My parents wrinkled their noses but didn't complain.

It was a little after five o'clock in the afternoon, near the end of February, when an ambulance brought Patrick home. It was snowing. I could see fat flakes of snow drifting aimlessly in the wedge of light under the street light. I stood in the front hall and watched two men carry a flat stretcher through the darkness, up our front walk, up the veranda steps and into the warmth of our house. Father closed the door after them but they seemed to have brought the cold in. I went up close to Patrick on the stretcher and said, "Hi, Patrick," in a voice that was too loud. My hands were cold and sweating at the same time. Patrick didn't say hi back. He lay on the stretcher bundled up like a mummy. I hadn't remembered his eyes being so big. He gazed at me almost with curiosity and then dismissed me by closing his eyes.

Patrick looked more dead than alive when they gently lifted him from the stretcher and settled him into his own bed. He was nearly as white as his sheets, a ghost come back to haunt our daredevil past. He barely made a dent in the pillows.

His room had a closed-up smell made perfumy by flowers and plants sent by family friends, former classmates, the Rotary Club and the I.O.D.E. All this had a numbing effect on me. It felt like a nightmare where you need to do something fast but you can only move in slow motion. I started babbling whatever came into my head, just to be doing something, just to break the crushing silence. "Hey, Patrick, looks like everyone in town sent flowers or a card."

"Big deal," Patrick said.

"Are you comfortable, dear?" Mother's voice had a guilty thinness which had never been there before.

"No." His voice was flat.

"Do you want another pillow?"

"Uh-uh."

Father's shoulders drooped. He looked more like someone accused than a judge. He seemed remote, unsure, as if he was unable to make a judgement about how a father behaved under these circumstances. Mother was pleating and unpleating the edge of the window curtain like a child waiting for someone to take charge. This was scary. Parents are supposed to know what to do next.

The doorbell rang and all of us, except Patrick, jumped. Like wind-up dolls Mother and Father moved towards the door at the same time. I was faster and swerved past them.

"Don't all get stuck in the door." Patrick's tone cut like a razor. Mother looked guilty again, and Father cross.

I ran downstairs, returning moments later with two boys,

classmates of Patrick's. I called out before I reached his bedroom, "Donald and Gerry to see you, Patrick."

Patrick closed his eyes, which was just as well. Both visitors stood open-mouthed, shocked by this scarecrow, this stick-boy lying motionless, his long-fingered hands useless as a doll's on top of the blanket. The boys regained a degree of composure, each mumbling hello. Patrick looked dead.

"Patrick," said Mother gently. The boys shuffled their feet and cleared their throats.

"Patrick, dear, open your eyes." She gave the boys an apologetic glance and smoothed his covers.

"Patrick!" Father was beginning to sound like a judge again.

Patrick opened his eyes and stared at an invisible spot on the wall. I took up babbling again in a nervous attempt to brighten the moment. "So, how's high school?" I asked the boys. Patrick should have entered first form with his friends the previous fall. I knew instantly it was the wrong topic. Father cleared his throat. Mother studied her hands.

Donald said, "Not bad," while at the same time Gerry said, "Not great." Gerry began to explain that the math was awful just as Donald jumped in all excited about basketball. He stopped suddenly. "It's only so-so, really." He seemed to have discovered a sliver in his thumb which needed his immediate attention.

Gerry frowned. "Basketball's great," he insisted. "We won the Junior. . . . " He too stopped short. "I mean, it's okay if you happen to like basketball." Patrick loved basketball.

There was another gap. Everyone just stood around breathing. Father was at the window now, studying the dark emptiness below. Mother was busy rearranging the flowers. She kept blinking.

"What else is new?" I was desperate.

"Not much." Gerry shrugged. "The girls are pretty old." Donald corrected him. "They're very mature."

"That too," Gerry agreed.

Patrick neatly ended the visit. "Thanks for coming, you guys." He glanced at his friends for one brief second, as if freezing them in time, and then closed his eyes.

The boys left Patrick's room with promises to return, but they looked at the floor when they said it. Downstairs they pulled on their toques and buttoned their jackets in silence. I watched them walk towards the street light. Donald kicked at a loose chunk of frozen snow and smashed it to smithereens.

The winds of early March moaned around our house, blowing in clouds heavy with freezing rain. I trudged to school through slush, learned more than I ever wanted to know about the parts of a flower and the effects of pollination, and slogged home again dreaming up ways to brighten Patrick's life. Daylight stayed with us a little longer now, and the sun put in an occasional appearance. Whenever it did, I could almost believe that April would come, and with it Easter — early this year — and the much-needed Easter holidays.

Nothing in our family was the same as it had been before Patrick's illness. It seemed that his personality was paralysed as well as his muscles, but we tried to smile even though, really, I think we all wanted to break down and howl. I wanted to shriek my head off and kick holes in walls. I didn't. We were all relatively quiet. Even Patrick didn't pout or cry or carry on. He might have been easier to deal with if he had. The problem was, he didn't react — to anything. He didn't seem to be in our world. Mother worked herself to a frazzle trying to comfort him. Father tried to jolly him up, then to reassure him that he understood. They both tried firmness. "You should be at your studies a little each day," Father told him, but got no response. "Nothing wrong with that brain of yours except lack of stimulation." Mother began reading to him from the first form history text, but she couldn't tell whether he was listening or thinking of something else. On our doctor's advice, they decided to give Patrick more time before making him do home studies. "He'll get around to it," the doctor said, "he's just taking a little longer to adjust."

He was taking forever to adjust. Nothing seemed to break through the wall Patrick was building between himself and the world — a world he needed, because he was as helpless as a baby.

It was worse at night. Sometimes I couldn't tell whether he was asleep or awake, and I know that was how he wanted it. Often, before I finally dropped off to sleep myself, I would get this sinking feeling, as if I were disappearing. I kept having the same dream that a great weight was holding me down, keeping me from moving. Every morning after the dream I had to crank myself up mentally, like the old gramophone we had down cellar, to make myself move faster, to be stronger, livelier. I needed extra life — enough for two. I was now a girl with a mission, a cause. I was Keely the Connor charging forward on my silver stallion to save my brother from... what? From despair? From losing hope in his future? The problem was that this cause was enormous. It was too big for me to handle all at once. I kept getting sidetracked and caught up in causes of lesser magnitude.

Patrick's bed, for instance. I badgered away at him until finally, worn down, I guess, he agreed to let me move it closer to the window. "I don't know what for," he grumbled while I tugged and pushed the blasted thing. "There's nothing to see in this dull neighbourhood." He was probably right. Bill pulling the breadwagon, its wheels back on, clip-clopping along the street. Not much excitement in that. The snow was nearly gone, except in shady areas; the grass was still a dirty brown. The street-sweeper came along with his wide broom, brushing the winter's sand and dried horse-droppings from the gutter. There was no hint of buds on the trees.

"Look!" I said. "In that big tree across the street. It's a... I think it's a vulture!"

Patrick looked. "It's a kite," he said dully.

"It looks like a vulture."

"It looks like a kite."

"That kite-shaped vulture looks like it's ready to swoop down on some poor murdered person lying under the hedge. See the feet sticking out?"

"Don't be . . . by golly, you're right. Those are feet."

We continued to watch and to speculate on the details. A shadow could have been a pool of blood. Something shaped a bit like a gun lay near the root of the tree — the discarded murder weapon. Then the feet moved. They were attached to legs which, in turn, were attached to Donald, Patrick's friend, winding up the kite string he had just disentangled from the bushes. "Why do I even listen to you?" Patrick sighed. He closed his eyes, dismissing me from his small world.

I couldn't blame him for being sullen. His illness had left him as powerless as a puppet with broken strings. There was no guarantee he would ever be able to walk, to catch a ball, to do up buttons. Some of his muscles worked a little bit, but he wouldn't use them. Soon they too would become flabby, from lack of exercise. The only thing he would do voluntarily was read his books. He had been given a book holder, which let him read by using a device attached to his head to turn pages. All his days were bad, but on his worst days he would neither read nor speak. In black silence he lay staring at some point on the wall opposite. I seemed to have more success than anyone getting him over his bad days. I nattered nonsense at him until he finally glanced at me. I asked stupid questions until he finally answered them just to shut me up.

The street lights had just come on, which was about as exciting as it was going to get.

"Is a spoon a boy or a girl?" I asked.

"For Pete's sake, Keely!"

"Which?"

"A girl."

"What's a knife?"

"A boy, I suppose."

"Then what's a fork?"

"Is this supposed to be a riddle?"

"No. I just like to think about things like this and I wondered if we still thought alike. What's a fork?"

Patrick paused for a moment. "A fork is a very old, old person, so old you can't tell whether it's male or female."

"That's sort of what I think, only I think a fork is in disguise so you can't tell." A whole five minutes had passed without Patrick staring into empty space. I turned on his lamp to cheer us up. "How would you paint summer?"

"How should I know?"

"I think it should be painted green."

"No," he said. "Yellow. Rosy yellow. All rounded and billowy."

"What about winter?"

"Straight lines. Black and white. . . spiky. With an orange sun going down." It could have been the lamplight, but Patrick seemed to have colour in his cheeks.

Tossing him questions didn't always work. Sometimes his mind seemed so deeply buried that he couldn't struggle back. He wouldn't say a word for hours. He would just look at me, his huge eyes the colour of black coffee in his ghost-white face.

Every day, walking home from school, Ginny asked about Patrick. I can't make my friendship with her sound logical. I could have pounded her when she used to brush me off like a pesky mosquito whenever Patrick was around. Now I'd have pulverized her if she'd lost interest.

"He can move a bit if he's in the right mood," I informed her. "One day he moved his arm as if he wanted to push me away. And he can move his head. He's supposed to do exercises, but he hates them. We're getting a nurse to look after him. He's too heavy for Mother."

We were in front of Ginny's. "How does Patrick like that idea?"

"Doesn't know yet. We've got two lined up to try out, one after the other. Whichever one Patrick hates the least is the one who gets the job. Come on over and say hello to him."

Ginny had heard about the reception Patrick had given Donald and Gerry and didn't know whether she had the nerve. "Tomorrow," she said.

I grabbed her by the coat and yanked. Ginny never buttoned her coat unless it was about ten below. She had a fate-worse-than-death look in her eyes.

"Ginny, he *needs* friends." I was pleading. "I think he's a lot better. Trust me. I promise he won't be scary." I crossed my fingers.

"You're just saying that."

"Would I lie to you?"

I went first into Patrick's room. It smelled like broken legs because he had plaster splints on his feet to prevent deformities. I thought I should warn him. "I have a surprise for you, Patrick!"

"I hate surprises," Patrick growled.

I bugled a fanfare and pulled Ginny through the doorway behind me.

Patrick's already pale face turned ashen. His eyes blazed as he threw the closest thing to a fit I had ever seen. "Go away!" he spat at Ginny. "Get out! Go away!" he screamed. In his fury he actually raised his head from the pillow.

Ginny and I clutched each other in terror. Ginny recovered enough to ask Patrick, "Why?"

"Because you're looking at me," he whispered, his eyes closed now.

"Why shouldn't I look at you? I like you."

"Well, I hate you. Get out!"

We both got out. Ginny cried; I cried. I started to go back in to Patrick but stopped. His chest heaved with silent despairing tears. The tears dried on his cheeks, eventually. He couldn't even wipe them away.

Downstairs Ginny blew her nose. "Well, that's it for Patrick and me," she said as I came down. "He hates me."

"He didn't mean it."

"He did so." Ginny looked as though the world had ended.

I didn't want the world to end, our Ginny-Patrick-Keely triangular world. I tried to make Ginny understand what Patrick was doing. "He's putting on an act, trying to invent a new personality."

"What was wrong with his old one?"

"Maybe he thinks it doesn't fit." Ginny looked puzzled. "With his new body. Come on," I said when she just shook her head, "we have to get him back. We have to do something."

Ginny looked away, but I saw her eyes fill up again. "Sure. I'll try to think of something, but.... " Her eyes drifted towards the stairs. "I didn't know he'd look like that. Why is he so thin? He looks as though he's ... disappearing."

"He is not disappearing!" I made my eyes glint. Ginny backed off. "His muscles may look as if they're disappearing because he can't use them. That's why he looks so thin. But there's more to a person than muscles, you know."

"I know. I didn't mean to.... "

"If you know, then you shouldn't sound so.... "

"Keely, you're beginning to be a bore."

"I don't care."

Near the front door, Ginny shrugged into her coat. She knotted her kerchief under her chin and pushed it back so it barely clung to the back of her head. Upstairs we could hear Patrick roaring for Mother. She came along the hall from the kitchen, head bent, and trudged up the stairs.

"I'll go, if you want," I called to her.

"No, I'd better." She continued up the stairs and then

began to hurry as Patrick's bellowing started a fit of strangled coughing.

Ginny's eyes sought mine. "I'll try to think of something," she whispered, hurrying out. "I mean it."

Mother was able to settle Patrick down, finally, with a small prescription pill from a pink box. The doctor had advised her to use the pills sparingly.

4

Mrs. Whinney arrived the following Monday. She was a matronly private-duty nurse with many years' experience. "Believe me," she said to my mother, "I've seen every ailment known to man. I've had patients as you'd never believe could live more than a week that'd hang on and hang on till the family would wish to heaven they'd gasp their last and be done with it." Mother and I turned startled eyes on each other.

"So this is the young lad, is it?" she said on meeting Patrick. "Well you're a poor, wizened, wee thing, aren't you, now, but you'll be light to pick up and that's a blessing."

Patrick closed his eyes.

Mrs. Whinney's first duty was to feed Patrick his dinner. When she came down to join the rest of the family in the dining-room she shook her head. "He won't last long, that lad. Eats like a bird."

My fork crashed down on my plate and everyone jumped.

After dinner Mother made a timid suggestion. "I'll get Patrick ready for bed tonight, Mrs. Whinney, if you would be good enough to help Keely do the dishes."

"It's a rare situation where the private nurse is called upon to do the household chores. It's not what I'm used to, Mrs. Connor, I don't mind telling you."

Father excused himself and went into the back parlour, with his hand squeezing his forehead. Domestic arrangements had begun to cause him severe, recurring headaches.

"Just for tonight," Mrs. Connor insisted, "until Patrick gets used to the idea of a nurse."

"Well, I'm sure you think you know what you're doing," Mrs. Whinney sniffed. "Far be it from me to interfere."

When the last dish was dried and put away in the cupboard, Mrs. Whinney heaved a put-upon sigh. "Just between you and me," she said, "that boy's spoiled rotten, the way he talks back and uses language that'd curl your hair." Mrs. Whinney's own hair had come out of its bun. She took a hairpin from the pocket of her apron and jabbed it into the twisted swag of greying hair which had come loose.

I glared at her. "He can't help it, you know."

"Oh, don't mind me, now. Goodness, you can't say a word around here but what you get your head chewed off by somebody. He'd be far better off in a Home, that lad, with other cripples around him. They'd have something in common. It might teach him a lesson to see somebody worse off than hisself. Take some of the misery out of him. Tell your mother I'd like a cup of tea in my room when she's not too busy."

To Mrs. Whinney's departing back I muttered, "Drop dead!"

Mrs. Whinney lasted only two days in our house.

Wednesday the new nurse arrived at our front door. Mother was drying a mixing bowl in the kitchen when the doorbell rang. She hurried to the door still drying the bowl and nearly collided with me. "Here, take these," she said. She looked nervous. She wiped her hands on her apron and went expectantly to the door. I placed the bowl on the hall table and threw the dishtowel in the same direction. The towel fell on the floor. Mother opened the door.

"You're going to have company," were Nurse Peggy Doyle's first words of greeting. She eyed the fallen towel.

Mother and I followed her gaze blankly. "If you drop a dish-towel, it means company's coming. That's what they say up home, anyway. Not that anyone believes it."

Crisp and starched in white uniform, white stockings and shoes, Peggy Doyle put her suitcase down in our front hall, her coat on top of it. Although she appeared to be a happy, hearty woman, I eyed her with distrust. Any nurse was suspect now, guilty of being Whinneyish until proven innocent. This one might possibly be a lunatic.

"Call me Peggy," she said to us on our way up to Patrick's room.

Patrick was prepared for this second attack on his privacy, eyes closed, mind apparently in reverse. Peggy took no notice of the awkward introduction. "I think someone's at your front door," she said, and a moment later the doorbell rang. Mother excused herself to answer the door. I hadn't heard anything before the bell sounded. I looked carefully at Peggy. Mother soon appeared in the doorway. "It's Mrs. Fisk from the Hospital Auxiliary. I can't very well leave her to. . . ."

"Don't worry," Peggy said, "it will give us time to steep."

Mother looked puzzled.

"Like tea."

"I see." Clearly she didn't. She scrutinized Peggy, and hesitantly left the room to go back to her caller.

Peggy began to walk about the room slowly. Occasionally she shook her head. Patrick opened his eyes to check on events but quickly closed them. I stood protectively beside his bed. Finally Peggy said, "There's something wrong here. There's a problem."

I couldn't keep exasperation out of my voice. "Of course there's a problem. The problem is, my brother is paralysed and he needs help." Patrick frowned but kept his eyes shut.

"Oh, him," said Peggy. "No, he's no problem. Not him. It's something else. This room is wrong. It's not right for him."

"It's my room," said Patrick, "and I'll stay here till the day

I die. Which," he added, "I hope will be soon."

Peggy said, "It's full of old lumber."

I sighed inwardly and shook my head. I had been right. A nutcase nurse.

Patrick opened his eyes. "Old lumber," he repeated with little interest. "Nothing but old furniture here."

Peggy opened his closet door and a hockey stick fell out. Peggy looked at it.

"That's hardly old lumber," I said.

Peggy put the hockey stick back and closed the door of the closet. "Bits and pieces," she said. "Remnants. You're still carrying them around and they're too heavy. Start again. Take up a new load, then go back and sort through your old lumber. There might be something you can use."

Patrick said, "I think you're a nutcase."

"Not at all. Let me see your hand." She picked up Patrick's hand, turned it over and brushed the fingers out nearly straight. She stared at it intently.

"You're a fortune-teller," I said, coming closer. "You read palms."

"Nonsense," Peggy scoffed. "I like to peek into people's lives a bit, that's all." She moved Patrick's hand and arm through a series of manipulations, bending and straightening his elbow, turning his hand palm up, then palm down, and raising his whole arm above his head. "Passive exercises," she said, answering the puzzled look on my face. Peggy moved around the bed and checked the palm of Patrick's other hand. Again she put his hand and arm through a series of movements. "So, do you paint pictures or write stories?" she asked Patrick.

"Get away from me," said Patrick. "You're a witch."

"I'm nothing of the sort. Surely you don't believe in witches at your age. I'm only an observer. You have a book-case full to overflowing with books and a smell of oil paint in your closet. My guess is that you're the creative type."

"I read a lot and I can't help how my closet smells."

"And look at the length of your ring finger."

In spite of himself Patrick raised his head half an inch from the pillow and glanced down at his hands, carefully placed, fingers outstretched on his top blanket. I looked too. "His fourth finger looks a bit long. Is that what you mean? Is that supposed to mean he's creative?"

"Oh, I wouldn't know," said Peggy. "Some people believe that, I suppose. Old wives' tale, probably."

"Patrick's an artist," I said.

Peggy looked surprised. "Is he?"

"Past tense," Patrick said.

"He specializes in horses."

"I used to."

Mother reappeared then, with a tea tray. "I made tea," she said, "but Mrs. Fisk couldn't stay." She poured tea into cups and placed a bent glass straw on the saucer of one. "She could only stay for a brief chat and to ask about you, Patrick."

"What does she want to know? When they're going to sign me up for the Montreal Canadiens?"

"Don't do that, Patrick." Mother looked as though she could easily cry. With an effort she brightened. "Mrs. Fisk passed along some news about Laurence Saunders' farm. Really, since Anita Fisk moved to town, Channing hardly needs a newspaper."

"What about the farm?" I asked. I was about to help Patrick drink his tea through the glass straw but Peggy took over.

"He sold it to people from Ottawa and bought Quinlan's Bakery. His farm is to be turned into a home for veterans."

"Veterans?"

"Soldiers," Patrick explained.

Mother continued. "Men wounded and needing some care, but not hospital care, apparently."

"What about the horses? Where will Bill and Lola live?"

"He won't need a horse. Mrs. Fisk said he bought a delivery truck. It's the end of an era," announced Mother. "And the beginning of a new way of life." She looked thoughtfully at Patrick.

"But," I insisted, "where will they go? The horses?"

"The glue factory, I expect," said Patrick.

"How can you say that? They're the only horses we know."

"Who cares? Horses are nothing but four-legged animals. Big deal. I'm not interested."

"But you used to. . . . "

"Used to," interrupted Patrick, "is the operative word." He gave a final suck on the straw and turned his head slightly away. Mother went downstairs to make more tea.

"What an interesting arrangement of tea leaves," Peggy said.

"Do you read tea cups, too?" I was becoming fascinated by Peggy.

"No, certainly not. Too much rigmarole to it. It's ridiculous. You're apparently supposed to turn the cup upside down in the saucer." She turned Patrick's cup upside down in the saucer. "And then I think you turn it three times and leave the handle pointing a certain way. And then. . . . " Peggy held the righted teacup in the palm of her hand at arm's length. She squinted at it with one eye. Twisting it, she half-closed her eyes and peered at it down her nose through her eyelashes. She brought it closer for minute inspection, turning it one way, twisting it another. She cocked her head on one side and said, "Ye-e-es." She tilted to the other side and said, "Mm-hmm."

"What?" I wanted to know.

"Shush," said Peggy. "Birds," she said after an eternity.

"Birds?" Patrick was becoming curious.

"Yes. Look here along the side." She showed the inside of

the teacup to Patrick. There was a scattering of wet tea leaves on one side, a dribble of smaller ones farther along, an intricate little design on the other side and several leaves in a clump adhering to the bottom of the cup.

"Birds in flight," explained Peggy. "One quite a bit larger than the other."

"What does that mean?" Patrick asked. "Am I going to turn into a bird and fly away, I hope?"

"Not exactly. But it could mean good news of some sort."

"That'll be the day!"

"There's something else here. It looks like a ship."

"Ah," said Patrick. "Drowned at sea. That sounds promising."

Peggy wasn't listening to him. "Or is it a chariot? It probably means a journey. An important journey. Very significant." She looked at Patrick over the teacup. I looked, too. Expectancy seemed to have replaced his former look of disdain. I went closer to look into the cup, but Peggy tilted it slightly towards herself. She frowned.

"There's something bad in there, isn't there," Patrick said watching Peggy carefully.

Peggy looked up. Still frowning, she peered intently at him. Very quickly she said, "I don't believe in bad fortunes. There's something else." Her expression cleared. "A package, possibly a gift. It's large, very large. See?" She pointed out a mass of leaves. "At any rate, it involves you intimately. It's something that affects your life."

"What life?" Patrick glanced at only a scattering of old tea leaves. The expectancy was gone. Mother had come in with fresh tea by this time. She smiled at the fortune-telling game. I wanted to know how Peggy did it.

"It's all a question of symbols," Peggy said, staring intently into the cup, her neck and shoulders tense.

"You haven't finished it," I said. "Do it all."

Peggy was silent. Suddenly, she shook her head rapidly. She put the cup on the bedside table with the saucer on top.

"I've done all I can do. It's given me a headache."

"Well, it's a very fine fortune all the same," said Mother. "Imagine, Patrick, a big surprise package to look forward to. I wonder what it could be?"

"Oh, probably a bike." Patrick closed his eyes.

CHAPTER

5

Every day I expected a huge package to be delivered for Patrick. Patrick expected nothing.

Whether or not to hire Peggy Doyle came to a family vote Sunday evening. Patrick's vote was an uncomplicated no. Mine was an emphatic yes. Mother wavered on the fence. She had no doubt about Peggy's nursing ability, but this tendency towards fortune-telling, no matter how much Peggy denied any real belief in it, was upsetting. Father reviewed the case for and against hiring Peggy and cast the deciding ballot. "She's helpful, she's cheerful, and from what I've seen, she knows her stuff," he said. "She can't help it if a little bit of the old magic and superstition still clings to her. She's from up the Valley, after all. It's bred into you up there. I say she stays."

Peggy was hired. I began to regret my vote while Patrick began to forget he had ever cast one. "She's nice and everything," I explained to Ginny, "but does she have to spend so much *time* with Patrick?"

"Well, she's his nurse."

"I know, but...."

"You're just jealous."

"I am not."

Patrick was unaware of the tension rising around him. Much of Peggy's time with him was spent bullying him into doing daily exercises. Although she wasn't a physiotherapist, she had worked side by side with physios and knew how to bend and straighten Patrick's arms and legs to keep his muscles toned up and to prevent contractures. "Look at it this way." She said this to me, although it was Patrick with his eyes closed she was aiming her lecture at. "Some of his muscles have nerve fibres regenerating, coming back to life, and some of his muscles don't because what they call the motor cells in his spine were wiped out by the polio germ. At this point we're not dead certain which muscle groups will come back, so we have to keep working them all. If we don't, his good muscles will atrophy, waste away. Some of his neck muscles are coming along. And so are some of his arm muscles. Patrick," she said, "push my hand away."

"Why should I?"

"To prove you can."

"Forget it. I can't." Patrick's arm was lying limply on the sheet. With one hand Peggy pressed lightly against his forearm. She stretched her finger over and tickled the inside of his wrist. "Quit it," Patrick said and moved his arm. I cheered; Peggy gloated and Patrick's mouth popped open. "Big deal," he said.

Every day I ran home from school to join in, to help out, but Patrick wouldn't let me lay a hand on him. I peered over Peggy's shoulder, dodged under her elbow to watch, but all I was was a fifth wheel. I needed an ally. "I'm going to invite Donald over to visit."

Patrick glared at me.

"What's wrong with that?"

After a long while he said, "My old life is dead, I know that. So. . . I want to be dead to my old friends. Don't bring them here to see me like this. I'm such a nothing."

I wanted to yell at him, to shake him. I couldn't. I couldn't even think of anything to say.

I tried luring him out of his despondency with tales of the

new neighbours on what had been Laurence Saunders' property. The people who were to run the Veterans' Home were Mr. and Mrs. Hodge. They had a daughter, Charlotte, a dimpled and fluffy-blonde girl about my age, and a ten-year-old son, Hartley. Hartley had the face of an angel and the habits of a gangster. He picked cigarette butts out of the gutter and smoked them. He lay on the cold, damp sidewalk so he could look up girls' skirts. I took the opportunity to kick him in the head one day, which made him scramble. He vowed to be my lifelong enemy. Fine with me, I told him.

Patrick was not intrigued. I told him about the renovations for the veterans, the ramps, the boardwalks, the extensions, but he was unmoved. I told him about Charlotte with her ruffles and bows and dimples. Patrick said dimples were kind of nice. "So's a bowl of rice pudding," I growled. I was envious. Secretly I poked my cheeks in, but no dimples formed. I told him about the horses. They were still there, bossy Lola (she'd lost her Lightning status) and old Bill. I had caught up with Laurence Saunders one day as he was coming out of the bakery and asked him about them. I hadn't seen them since midwinter.

"Sold 'em along with the farm," he said. "The Hodges are hiring a young lad to keep an eye on them. Surprised you haven't seen him. Hodge put an ad in the paper and this lad answered it. He's about your age, maybe a little older. Goes to the high school. He has a horse of his own he wants to board there."

"He has a horse of his own?" The boy began to grow in importance. What kind of boy would own a horse, I wondered. A prince, possibly. Or someone very princelike. A prince in disguise. "If you see this guy," I said to Laurence, "tell him I'd give anything to ride his horse. I'd even take another whack at Lola, as far as that goes."

"Sure, I'll tell him. It's young Alex Dalby I'm talkin' about. Lost his dad overseas. His mother sold the farm and moved to town. Young lad wouldn't part with his horse, I guess. He's to work weekends and in the holidays, helping out with the vets. It's a lucky break for Mrs. Dalby. The money, I mean. Their farm didn't fetch much. I was lucky." He smiled and tipped his hat. A businessman now, he no longer wore a tweed cap. "Give my regards to your brother," he said. "A harsh blow. Such a harsh blow." He shook his head sympathetically.

All the way home I thought about Alex Dalby with a horse of his own, a horse he kept right behind our backyard. No reason I couldn't do the same. Anybody could get a horse. Probably. You didn't have to be a prince. I had seventeen dollars in a box in the back of the second drawer of my desk. Maybe not enough for a horse, at least not a very good horse, but it was a start. I could save my allowance, my birthday money, give up a few things like the show on Saturdays. Unless they were playing movies about horses.

I told Patrick about the boy with the horse and about my plans to buy one of my own. He closed his eyes and frowned. He made it pretty clear that he wasn't interested.

Peggy seemed to have better luck breaking through Patrick's barrier. In the late afternoon she lit the lamp in his room. She sat in a rocking-chair which she had begged from the living-room and which Mother was glad to see the end of, knitting endless sleeves and backs of sweaters and talking about the war. She had spent a year overseas in a London hospital looking after amputees. Now, after the four o'clock bell, I rushed away from the schoolyard din to be a part of the atmosphere she was creating. I always looked up at the glow in Patrick's window as I came rushing along the street. It made me feel. . . homesick. I endured school. I only came to life in Patrick's room.

Inside, I raced upstairs, kicked off my shoes and huddled on the end of Patrick's bed. At first he didn't seem to notice. As he began to listen to Peggy's stories, though, he became aware of me. "Off," he ordered. "You're unbalancing me." I had to drag a small wicker chair into Patrick's room from mine. His room was beginning to look like a used furniture dealer's storeroom.

I had given up resenting Peggy. It's hard to be curious about someone's real-life stories and jealous at the same time. Even though he rarely responded, I knew Patrick was listening. He would shift his gaze from time to time, instead of staring vacantly at an invisible spot on the wall. I had to interrupt Peggy and ask questions for both of us.

"Weren't you afraid of the bombs?"

"Yes, terrified."

"What made you decide to go over there?"

"Oh, well, I. . . . " For the first time since we had known her, Peggy seemed unnerved, at a loss for words. She took a breath and went on. "I went over to look for my fiancé." She looked at her watch and started to get out of the rocking chair. "Nearly dinnertime," she said.

"No, wait!" I pressed her back down. I had drawn up my chair as close as possible to hers so as not to miss a word. "What do you mean, to look for your fiancé? Did you already have one who was lost, or were you trying to find one?"

Peggy hesitated. "Lost," she said.

I inched closer, looking intently into Peggy's face. I sensed something here. A true story; a true romance. I specialized in making discoveries about people, mysterious romantic discoveries. Then I made up what-if stories about them and told them to myself at night when I couldn't get to sleep. Sometimes I couldn't get to sleep because my stories were too exciting — especially when I starred in them, solving the mysteries and saving everybody from the jaws of death.

I begged Peggy to go on with her story.

She sighed as though she might as well get it over with. "We were engaged to be married," she began, "just before he went overseas. About six months later I received a telegram saying he was missing and presumed dead." She stopped.

"Oh, no!" I said. Peggy was busy counting stitches. If I'd been making up the story I might have said missing, but not dead. I wouldn't have brought dead into it at all. I looked at Patrick. He looked upset too. We waited for the story to go on. It didn't.

I tried to get my face between Peggy's and her knitting. "And so you wept," I prompted.

"Well yes, of course." She started counting her stitches out loud. "Thirty-two, thirty-three. . . . "

"You were stricken with grief." I needed details.

"Well, I. . . . "

"You vowed then and there to leave not a stone unturned as you searched the world for your lover!"

Patrick spoke. "Keely, for Pete's sake!"

"You certainly lead a rich and satisfying fantasy life, Keely, my dear," said Peggy.

"Well, somebody has to!"

"Yes," Peggy continued, "I went over to look, not expecting to find him, really, but not exactly believing he was dead. I didn't have the right sense of loss. It was only a hunch, a feeling, mind you."

Patrick and I exchanged a glance. "Yes, that's it," I said. "Because of your. . . sixth sense. . . you knew."

"No, it was just a hunch."

"And then what?"

"I didn't find a trace of him. The war ended and I came home." She got up at that point and squeezed past my wicker chair. Lines creased her forehead.

"But what's his name? What does he look like?"

"End of story," Peggy said crossly and went downstairs.

"Holy!"

"Now look what you did!" Patrick sounded disappointed. "You shouldn't have pumped her. You made her cross."

I ignored him. I had something to think about. "Obviously we have to find her dead soldier. This is our mission."

"For Pete's sake, Keely! He's dead."

"He's not dead. If Peggy believes he's alive, he's alive. If anyone would know, Peggy would, wouldn't she?"

"She said it was only a hunch."

"Yes, but for Peggy I think a hunch is a sure bet."

"She was pretty worked up," Patrick reflected. "If it was really 'end of story', why would she get so huffy with us?"

"Because," I said, "she probably has a hunch about us, too." I looked Patrick in the eye. His gaze didn't waver from mine. "We are the ones!"

"You mean, she thinks we're going to find him." It wasn't a question. Slowly, and with significance, I nodded.

Something of Patrick's old intensity hovered. He seemed trapped in a dream. "Can you imagine a paralysed hero?"

"Yes," I said. "I can. If anyone can bring Peggy's dead soldier back to life, a paralysed hero can."

"I would say," said Patrick, "it's symbolic." He seemed lost in a dream tinged with hope.

"Definitely."

I still looked forward to Patrick's surprise package every day, and every day nothing continued to show up. Hopeful buds began to appear on the trees, encouraged by the sun's first warmth. Lola mooched about now, on the slope of the high pasture, and occasionally Bill. I had yet to glimpse the horse belonging to Alex Dalby, the prince in disguise. What sort of horse would he have? An ivory and black piebald or a mighty black stallion? I hoped the former. Velvet Brown was my kind of person. I reread both *National Velvet* and *The Black Stallion* and memorized bits of each to get in shape for flying over the high pasture. I knew exactly how to do it. It was all so easy. Just a question of having a horse. Every week I deposited most of my allowance into the box in the second drawer of my desk.

Charlotte Hodge, whose parents ran the Veterans' Home, had taken to walking home from school with Ginny and me. Although she was the same age, she was a grade behind. We were both in the entrance class, looking longingly towards first-form high school next year.

"They'll probably skip me pretty soon," Charlotte told us. "School's really simple here, compared to Ottawa." Ginny and I exchanged glances. We scuffed along the street, not saying much. Charlotte looked down at my shoes. "Do you still have to wear Oxfords with toe-caps? In Ottawa only little kids wear those." I watched her trip along, daintily pointing the toe of her brand-spanking-new white sandal with a heel that was ever so slightly high. Even if I had white sandals, even if I *wanted* white sandals, my mother would never have let me wear them before the twenty-fourth of May — for reasons, I imagine, best known to my mother. I gave Charlotte a sidelong look and thought, what if we had an earthquake right now and Charlotte fell in?

I came in from school to find Mrs. Fisk of the Hospital Auxiliary having tea with Mother. "Hi," I said from the doorway of the living-room. Mother squinted the corners of her eyes at me and I added, "Hi, Mrs. Fisk." Mother always has these rules. . . .

Mrs. Fisk said, "My soul-and-body, how you've grown! Quite the young lady."

I gave her a lips-only smile, about to back out, but she patted the couch cushion beside her. Mother squinted sweetly at me again so I was forced to sit. I refused tea. Politely.

"Well, as I say, we were all simply flabbergasted." Mrs. Fisk seemed to have lost interest in me and my height and my young ladyness. She went on talking to my mother. "Just through an ad in the paper. Anyone knowing the whereabouts of Lance Corporal James Fisk. . . that sort of thing. And not two months later who should arrive on my brother-in-law's doorstep but the young lad himself."

I was probably staring at Mrs. Fisk with my mouth open, because she said to me, "Missing in action, you know."

I said, "Gosh!"

"He was altered, mind you, quite altered."

"How come?"

"Keely. . . ." Mother was squinting warningly at me now. Mrs. Fisk continued. "Shell-shock, they say. But still, can you imagine? Through an ad in the paper!"

"Some people are just plain lucky, I guess," Mother said.

"Yes indeed." Mrs. Fisk looked at my mother and looked down at her teacup. "We could all use a bit of luck, couldn't we?"

"Keely," Mother interrupted, "perhaps you should get at your homework." I jumped up, relieved of my social duty, and started upstairs, thinking that the words "shell-shock" had an interesting ring to them.

"With any luck at all," I heard Mrs. Fisk say, "things will start looking up for your poor lad." I stopped at the bottom of the stairs.

"I hope you're right. What you're doing is wonderful, Anita," Mother said. "We're very appreciative."

"We all agreed it was a worthy project," Mrs. Fisk replied. "Of course, we'll need specific measurements."

Mother paused. "That may be difficult to arrange and still keep it a secret, but we'll manage somehow."

"Keep what a secret?" I asked, after Mrs. Fisk had gone.

"It wouldn't be a secret if I told you, would it?" She was being maddening.

I pounded up to Patrick's room. Patrick was reading, his book attached to its special holder. Peggy sat in the rocker knitting. I dropped my book bag on the floor, making them both jump. "What's this about a secret?" I demanded.

Patrick continued to read. Peggy looked up sharply from

her knitting. She glanced at Patrick and gave me a glaring, head-shaking look I didn't understand.

"What's going on, Peggy?"

Peggy rolled her eyes to the ceiling and shook her head again. "Haven't the foggiest," she said.

I watched her suspiciously. Peggy pulled a long strand of wool from the yellow ball which, inch by inch, was being devoured by the clicking jaws of her knitting needles. Inch by inch it appeared reincarnated as the sleeve of a sweater. She said she had knit all through the war and couldn't get out of the habit. I hunched down in my wicker chair. "Why am I always the outcast in this family? No one ever tells me anything."

"I'm sure all will be revealed in good time," said Peggy. "Don't destroy the chair, Keely dear."

I was picking off loose bits of wicker. "No one trusts me." I got up and paced the floor. I rubbed my nose and thought, what if the floor gave way right under Peggy?

"Get a handkerchief, Keely," Peggy said.

"I don't need one. My nose is itchy."

"Oh-oh. That means you're going to kiss a fool."

"Does it?" I asked. Patrick looked up from his book. I smooched out my lips and leaned threateningly over him.

"Help! Get her away from me. She's making me throw up."

"Keely!"

"Can't anyone take a joke around here? Am I that repulsive?"

"Yes," said Patrick, closing his eyes.

I slouched against the window-sill. "Everyone hates me, obviously."

"Nearly thirteen," said Peggy, "is a difficult age." She pulled another long strand of wool free. "You've got the tail-end of childhood dragging behind you and the tough end of young womanhood stretched out in front of you. Straighten up, Keely. Don't slouch like that or they'll be putting you in a back brace."

I stood up straight, hunching up my shoulders, thrusting out my chin. I was tall for my age. My dream was to look older and more dramatic. I said, "I left childhood behind ages ago." I was thinking of the day I had fallen off Lola and Patrick had saved me from having my head kicked in. The day Patrick got sick was the last day of my childhood, as far as I was concerned.

"You should practise walking with a book on your head, child, for your figure."

"Child! Why does everyone treat me like a kid? No one tells me anything, they keep secrets from me, they act like I'm a moron. . . . "

"Maybe it's just that you're a little impetuous," she suggested.

"What's that got to do with anything?" I wasn't about to ask what impetuous meant. I glared at her. "You're as bad as everyone else. I ask a few simple questions about your fiancé and you walk out as if I've insulted you."

"Now, Keely." Peggy put her knitting down. "I know what you're like. If I even so much as told you he was tall you'd be out looking for him, scouring the streets, questioning everyone in uniform over six feet. I wouldn't put it past you to go to Ottawa and check at National Defence Headquarters."

"Hey, that's an idea." I was cheering up. "Have you done that?"

"Keely! See what I mean? You're impetuous."

"No, I'm not. I just like to get to the middle of things fast. If you'd only trust us with some details, Patrick and I could find him."

Patrick groaned. "You're spoiling it, Keely. Can't you just grow up?"

"Grow up!" I was angry now.

"You heard me! You don't solve mysteries by putting your head down and ramming at them. And anyway, it wasn't for real. It was supposed to be. . . symbolic." His voice dropped and he glanced quickly at Peggy and away, embarrassed. He frowned at me.

"I don't understand," Peggy said.

"I understand perfectly," I said. "Patrick thinks I'm a jerk and he hates me. Fine then. See if I ever darken your doorstep again." I gathered up my book bag and slammed out of Patrick's room. Peggy called after me, but I didn't answer. I had declared war. On the whole world. I put my head down and rammed my way into my room.

The next day, Saturday, nothing changed. The sky was leaden, as was my heart. Mother and Peggy were quietly planning something in the kitchen but changed the subject when I came in. I went out. I phoned Ginny, but she sounded funny. She was being evasive. I never beat around the bush. "What's up?" I asked her.

"Nothing much," Ginny hedged.

"Gin-n-ny!"

Ginny sighed. "Carol Katski asked me over, and Buddy Dolan, and I said I'd go."

I didn't say anything.

"It's a free country," she added.

"Fine then."

"I'll get Carol to ask you too."

"Don't bother. I hate Buddy Dolan and anyway, I'm busy." I hung up a little more firmly than was necessary.

I got out my roller-skates and clanged them together to knock off the dust. I didn't really want to roller-skate, but I didn't want to hang around the house either, being a friendless, untrusted, childish outcast. When I was eleven I asked for boxing gloves for Christmas and got roller-skates instead. They were good skates, the best, but they weren't boxing gloves. How could my parents think they were interchangeable? Sometimes I just felt like punching something, but instead I roller-skated, came home, took off my skates — and still felt like punching something.

I skated down the street towards the new Veterans' Home and toyed with a what-if story. What if, just at the corner, a Russian spy in a big, black limousine stopped, yanked me inside and held me hostage. But little did he know I had unusual powers. With superstrength I ploughed him one with my skates, grabbed the steering wheel and raced the car downtown to the police station, right beside the court-house where my father just happened to be coming out and my mother, by chance, was shopping nearby and. . . .

A boy (it had to be the horse boy) stood at the end of the lane to the Veterans' Home, nailing a sign to the maple near the road. He whacked in the last nail and stood back from his handiwork. I was close enough to see that the sign read Sunny View Acres. He heard me rattling along, looked at me and sort of nodded before starting up the lane. I was left with my mouth hanging ready to say something like "Great day for a horseback ride." It didn't actually look like a great day for anything. It was about to pour down rain. "Hi!" I called hopefully to his back.

"G'day," he called back over his shoulder. He didn't stop to chat about horses.

G'day, I mimicked silently. What a drip!

This section of Fairly Street had been freshly blacktopped not long ago. You could still catch a whiff of the hot, sharp smell of tar. It was almost as smooth as skating on the kitchen linoleum, which I used to do sometimes when Mother was out. Charlotte's brother, Hartley, came skulking down the lane now, smirking at me with his pink choirboy mouth and glancing around, probably checking to see if I had any bodyguards with me. I didn't. Didn't need any. He slithered down and squatted under the sign on the tree, without taking his eyes off me. His hair was brushed into a kewpie-doll wave over his forehead.

I decided to ignore him.

"Hey, kid," he yelled as I wheeled close, "get off my road."

"You don't own it." I sped past.

"Do so."

"Do not." I skated back to the corner, let a car pass and skated down the middle, where it was smoothest of all. I stuck my leg out behind and, with arms spread, pretended I was

Barbara Ann Scott, Canada's own darling on figure-skates. I felt a few drops of rain but I didn't care.

"Hey, beanpole, get your carcass off my road!"

"Make me, snake-face," I yelled, with both feet back under me. Hartley lunged, but I swerved and skated on. Back I came again, taunting him, daring him. Again he missed. I watched him steal away up the lane towards his house and thought he must have given up. What a disappointment! There had been something bracing in this skirmish. I didn't want to win the battle by default. I was after blood. And besides, he'd started it. I skated up to the end of the fresh paving again, turned in front of an oncoming car and, when the driver honked his horn, made a face. What a vicious place the world was! It began to rain in earnest now.

I didn't see Hartley behind the parked car. The wind rushing past my face made my eyes water and deafened me. At that moment I knew I was *faster than a speeding bullet, more powerful than a locomotive, able to leap tall....* Then Hartley Hodge leaped out from behind the parked car and spilled a juice can of gravel in my path.

There was blood, all right, but it was from my own torn knees and the palms of my hands. One of my skates came off; the strap had broken. I grabbed the skate and leaped to my feet faster than a speeding bullet, surprising Hartley. He was backed up against the parked car, which allowed him no escape. He ducked and dodged, but I was both taller and quicker. I grabbed him by the shirt-front with one hand, twisting it into his neck, and raised the skate over his head. A tortured, gurgling snort came from his blocked windpipe. The rain stood out in beads on his greased-up kewpie-doll wave. There was a low, threatening roll of thunder. "I could bust in your stupid, baby-doll face, you know," I panted. His eyes, alert to the threat, were little black circles of fear. He was waiting for the blow. I raised the skate higher for greater impact and suddenly a what-if scene came over me, unasked for. What if this CCM Sunshine steel roller-skate, more dangerous at the moment than boxing gloves, flattened the kid. What if he lay on the road helpless as a baby. For ever. I couldn't wish that on even my avowed, lifelong enemy. Almost too fast for thought, I saw Patrick's dark defeat in this boy's eyes. I loosened my grip on the neck of his shirt and watched his eyes ice over as he realized he was home free. I gave him a shove and he scuttled away to the safety of his lane.

I pushed off on my one skate towards home, rain streaming down my face. Maybe I should have, I kept thinking, maybe I should have. On the other hand, what if his mother was fond of him?

6

Once home, I limped up the driveway, one shoe, one skate, undid the remaining skate and deposited them both in a trunk in the garage. Rain pelted the garage roof. The trunk held other remnants of childhood: the bobskates I first clacked around on on the rink Father made us when we were little; two thick double-dutch ropes I'd had since grade three, which older girls used to ask to borrow (a small thing, but it had boosted me up a rung above the "little kids"); a Laura Secord box containing coloured bits of broken hopscotch glass, including my lucky red one shaped more or less like a diamond; and, finally, the brown corduroy bag, with a drawstring, made by my mother for holding my marbles. Ginny kept hers in a dark blue bag that said Crown Royal on it, which I coveted but which my father said wasn't quite the thing because of the position we all had to uphold on account of him being a judge. Anyway, there was my childhood in the trunk, my roller-skates plunked on top. I closed the lid. In a few months I would be a teenager seeking higher things in life. I was just getting a jump start on it, that's all. I wished I could lock the trunk, but there was no key. I was a little afraid I might be lured back to childhood even though I knew my best course of action was to plunge forward into adulthood.

It wasn't that I was so keen on being old; I just wanted to be taken seriously. I wanted to be trusted with secrets. Mostly, I suppose, I wanted Patrick to have faith in me. I wanted him to say, "You're right, Keel, there's more to a person than muscles. I think I'll get on with my life."

At dinner I put on an impressive display of maturity — napkin in my lap, elbows off the table, passed things without being asked. Mother, Father, even Peggy, just took it all for granted. I needed to make a bigger, more adult impression. I offered to do the dishes by myself.

"I was just going to suggest that," my mother said. "My back has been bothering me today. I thought I'd lie down."

She didn't say, "How overwhelmingly adult of you to offer." Nobody did. I leaned against the sink and sloshed the dishcloth lightly over the dishes. It was unfeeling of her to take me up on my offer. Maturity is one thing, but slave labour is not what I'd had in mind.

A little later Ginny phoned, I guess to make up for not hanging around with me all day. She invited me over. The evening was musky with the smell of damp earth. Fallen leaf-bud casings squished underfoot like caterpillars.

"Buddy Dolan is a drip," was the first thing Ginny said when we were safely up in her room, "and so is Carol Katski."

Sitting on Ginny's bed, I crossed one banged-up knee over the other and made a dramatic pooh-pooh gesture with my hand. "Ginny," I said, "I've grown beyond all that."

"Huh?" enquired Ginny. She was staring at my one knee crossed over the other, not because of the wad of bandage I'd taped to it after I'd wrecked it roller-skating, but because we both think crossed knees look so affected. We used to, that is.

"I've put childhood behind me." I hoped I could sell the same idea to Ginny because I could hardly be expected to hang around with someone who was still a mere child, and Ginny was, after all, in spite of Carol Katski and Buddy

Dolan, my best friend.

"Why?" Ginny asked.

"You probably wouldn't understand."

"Give me a hint."

I hesitated. "I have important things to do." I was speaking very calmly, very maturely and a little mysteriously.

"Such as?"

"I . . . I want to help Patrick find Peggy's dead soldier."

"What's the point?"

"It's symbolic."

"Oh, symbolic." Ginny was still having trouble with symbolic, it seemed, judging from her blank expression.

"And I want people to trust me with secrets."

"I don't get it. What secrets?"

"And I want to save Patrick."

"From what?"

"From disappearing."

"Keely . . . you know, sometimes you're half-cracked."

"I know. But Patrick has always wanted to be a hero, and I've always wanted to be a hero too."

"Heroine," Ginny corrected me.

"No, not a heroine," I scoffed. "What do they do? Just sit around looking dull all day while the hero gets to go out and rescue everybody." I was thinking of Roy Rogers, the Lone Ranger, all the Saturday afternoon cowboys. "Nope, I'd rather be a hero. A mature, womanly hero, just going about my business getting everything fixed up. Oh, I've left childhood far behind, Ginny. What you're looking at is a woman."

Ginny stared. "You don't *look* a whole lot different."

I stood now in front of Ginny's dressing-table mirror, Ginny beside me, and brooded on my own reflection, my dark, deep-set eyes and black eyebrows. My dark hair, cut bluntly, fell forward around the prominent bones of my face. Beside me Ginny shone like the sun, reddish highlights in her short curls, an artistic sprinkling of freckles.

Ginny said, "I think you'd be more believable if you wore your hair in an upsweep." She illustrated this by grabbing handfuls of my hair and sweeping it back away from my face.

I studied the effect. "Yes, I see what you mean."

"You need to look a bit Joan of Arc-ish."

Over the bookcase in Mr. Leach's classroom were pictures of heroes and martyrs, Joan of Arc among them, her hair clipped as short as a man's, her face purely, bravely aglow. Ginny let my hair fall back into place and Joan of Arc disappeared. In her place was Keely Connor, peering out from under a hedge of hair.

Spring was making definite inroads and hinting at warmer days to come. The robins were back. I had caught glimpses after school of one or other of the veterans walking, sometimes with Charlotte Hodge looking important, or being pushed in a wheelchair by Alex Dalby, the hired boy. It had occurred to me that the place to start looking for Peggy's dead soldier was right here. Soldiers, obviously, would know soldiers. I mentioned this to Patrick.

He had lost most of his earlier enthusiasm. "You don't know his regiment. You don't know his rank. You don't even know his name, for crying out loud. How can you expect . . . ?"

"That's where you come in," I interrupted. "Peggy likes you. She trusts you. Find out everything you can, and if possible get her to show you a picture of him."

"Come on, Keely, this is only a pipe dream. Why are we doing this?"

"For Peggy's sake. So she can marry him and live happily ever after."

"And if that happens, what will become of me? They'll get old Whinney back, or somebody even worse. I'll be like a rag doll handed on from one nurse to the next."

"By the time all this comes about, I may well be completely grown up. I'll look after you."

"Not on your Nellie." Patrick closed his eyes.

"Patrick!" I prodded him. "You know why we're doing this. It's our destiny."

"Fairy-tales, Keel."

"Don't forget Peggy's hunch. About us."

Patrick's eyes drifted lazily open.

"This is no ordinary hunch." My eyes burned into his. "Don't forget," I said, "this is symbolic." I had Patrick's attention. "Now, here's the plan. You can be the brains behind this search and I'll do the legwork."

"Seems a fair division of labour so far."

"I'm not kidding." I waited for Patrick to show some interest.

At last he said, "Okay, I'll see what I can find out."

Sunday afternoon I went out to look for the first trilliums at the edge of our property. I knew it was way too early, but I like to get on with things. Instead of trilliums I found the long-awaited horse nibbling bits of new grass, with his nose under the fence between our place and Sunny View Acres. He was neither a black stallion nor a piebald, but a bay with a coat like polished mahogany and a black mane and tail. I reached out and scruffed the bridge of his nose. He pushed his head over the fence searching for treats so I ran inside to get him a carrot. I returned to find Alex standing beside his horse. His own horse!

"Hi," I said, puzzling over his too-short overalls, his faded checked shirt and the straw fedora pulled down so far onto his head that his ears stuck out. If he was a prince in disguise, the disguise was working. "I'm a friend of Laurence Saunders," I began. "Last summer he let me ride his. . . ."

"I know," said the hayseed prince. "You're the kid I'm supposed to teach how to ride. Laurence told me about you."

Had Alex called me a kid? "I know how to ride," I said quickly, maybe a little too quickly. "I just don't know how to jump."

"Jump!"

"Jump."

"Laurence said you fell off."

This farm lad was beginning to use up my patience. I gave a large sigh to let him know this. I propped one foot on the fence and gazed unconcernedly off over my left shoulder at a patch of early dandelions. "Look, if you don't want me to ride your horse, just say so. I know plenty of other people with horses." He didn't say anything so I looked at him. He was sizing me up with narrowed eyes, so I added, "But I don't know them all that well."

"Okay," he said. "If jumping's what you want, that's what it'll be. This height suit you?" He indicated something about shoulder high.

"On second thought. . . ." I tried to get my voice out of the panic range. "On second thought, let's just concentrate on plain riding, no jumps."

Alex began to lead his horse towards the stable. "Come on," he said over his shoulder. High up in the pasture, Lola and Bill stood nose to tail. I climbed the fence and ran after Alex and his horse. Lola gave a long whicker of derision. Bill merely nodded his head.

Alex called his horse Ginger, I discovered, and Ginger seemed to know what was expected of him in the saddling-up department. He could have been a horse straight out of one of my books. With some dismay I noticed Charlotte hopping off her porch and coming our way, looking both cute and friendly. She perched delicately on the fence to watch.

Alex stood back from his horse. "Okay," he said to me, "she's all yours. Let's see you do your stuff."

I pulled myself up very straight, the way Peggy was always after me to do, and strode towards Ginger. A drum roll was going on inside me but it may only have been my heart pounding. My mouth went dry. I was on Ginger's right side but I climbed up into the saddle anyway, forgetting rule number one: Always mount from the left. Ginger danced sideways and Alex shook his head in disbelief. "What do you do for an encore?" he asked.

Charlotte tittered.

I didn't like his tone. I didn't have to take that. "Giddy-up," I said to Ginger. Ginger only flicked his tail. I shook the reins and Ginger shook his head. Alex began to whistle "Yankee Doodle", and Charlotte hummed along, just to be annoying. I was very erect in the saddle and more than dignified. Madly, I turned horse-book pages in my mind. How to make them go? You'd think I'd have read it in chapter one — although I tend to skip chapter ones if they only give boring directions. I jerked forward in the saddle two or three times to give the horse the right idea. It didn't work.

"Maybe if you stand on your head and spit nickels. . . ."

Charlotte brayed in appreciation of Alex's humour.

I threw each of them a withering glance through half-shut eyes. "I've changed my mind. I'd rather not ride today." Why was I saying this? I wanted to ride today and every day. I wanted to be an expert by the time I got a horse of my own.

"Suit yourself." Alex looked unconcerned.

"Why don't we all play Chinese checkers, then?" Charlotte suggested. I made a little gagging sound in my throat for Charlotte's benefit and slipped down from the right (always dismount from the left) side. I left the reins dangling (never leave the reins etc.) and walked *behind* (huge mistake) the horse. Ginger knew the rules and gave me a swift kick in the knee to tell me so. I yelped like a wounded animal and leaped for safety.

Alex held back his laughter. He tucked his hands into his armpits as if to keep from doubling over and pointing at me. Charlotte gave a little scream and covered her mouth, giggling behind her hands.

"You okay?" Alex had the decency to ask.

"Of course." I tried not to wince.

"Well, I'll tell you," Alex said, and there was sympathy in his voice, "there's only one thing worse than being kicked by a horse."

"What?" I couldn't imagine anything worse.

"Being bitten by a horse."

"Oh." I remembered Lola's big, yellow teeth. Not a pleasant prospect.

"And the only thing worse than that is being stabbed in the back by your best friend. Now watch." With few words but plenty of action, he showed me my mistakes and how to correct them. I watched him mount, dismount, start (you nudge the horse with your heels), stop, turn right, then left. Finally I watched him take off at full gallop. By the time he came flying back across the field, I saw him in a different light. I admired him. More than admired him. He drew up to where I stood. My injured knee was forgotten. Maybe he was wearing worn overalls and an Old Macdonald hat, but what I saw now was something like a fur-trimmed cape flung back from his shoulders. His satin breeches gleamed in the afternoon sunlight. I thought he brushed princely golden locks away from his eyes as he handed me the reins.

"Holy!" I said.

"See," Charlotte said, "that's how you're supposed to do it." She was still clinging securely to the fence.

Rule number one. I placed my foot in the left stirrup. The lessons went well, slowly — no galloping, but on the whole a very satisfactory afternoon. When it was over and we were rubbing Ginger down I asked Alex where he had got such a smart horse.

"My father," was all he said.

I wanted him to go on, to answer how come and when and where and describe what was said to whom and by whom. A two-word answer doesn't make a story. So I . . . encouraged him. Pumped him, Patrick would have said. His father had grown up with horses in England, apparently. He'd wanted Alex to have the same experience even though they could barely afford it. "My father was a dreamer, not a farmer," he said as he turned Ginger out into the high pasture.

"Why was that?"

"What difference does it make now?" He stood looking sadly towards the grassy hill. He straightened his shoulders then and abruptly took off, muttering, "I've got work to do." He wasn't an easy person to figure out.

I could tell by the sun that it was late. I'd deserted Patrick for the entire afternoon. I'd make it up to him, entrance him with stories about riding, about Alex, about Alex's father the dreamer. There was scope here for some good what-ifs.

I was stiff and bow-legged but I could still race upstairs to Patrick's room. "Guess what?" I shouted, rounding the doorway and flinging myself into my wicker chair.

"I don't want to hear about it." Patrick's voice was lifeless.

"But, Patrick, I rode, I actually, professionally rode a horse. A good horse. I wasn't flying, exactly. I'll probably learn that next Sunday."

"Quit it. Shut up. I'm not listening."

Patrick had been alone all afternoon. It was Peggy's day off. He lay propped on his pillows, wan, thin, his eyes deepened by dark shadows. I calmed down and said I'd bring his dinner.

"I don't want any."

Now I regretted my enthusiasm. Why did I always have to make such a big deal out of everything? I should have just talked about the weather, the sunshine, the robins. I sat on the side of Patrick's bed. "You have to eat."

"Says who?"

"You'll get sick."

"Good."

I started to object to his attitude but bit my tongue. I

couldn't say anything to change it that he hadn't heard before. In silence we watched the afternoon's glow deepen slowly into evening's gloom.

Patrick's obsession with sickness and death made me feel as though I were being twisted, wrung out like a wet towel. I didn't think I had enough joy of my own left to share with him. I couldn't blame him. Who wouldn't have trouble coming to terms with his problems — a lively mind and memory, but useless arms and legs? We all desperately loved him and looked after his needs, but he required something beyond that.

It came to me as vividly as the lightbulb you see over somebody's head in a comic book. He needed a friend. Someone brand-new. I bounced slightly on Patrick's bed to get his attention. "You need a friend," I said.

"Like a hole in the head."

"A chum. A boy your own age."

"Don't be ridiculous."

"Yes." A plan was developing. The lightbulb blazed in my brain. "Leave it to me. I think I can work something out."

"Just don't. I know what'll happen. You'll ram ahead with some half-baked idea that'll end up being embarrassing for all concerned. Especially me."

"I won't ram ahead. I don't do that any more. I'll bide my time. Just bide my time." I rose from the side of the bed and, deep in thought, walked slowly from the room.

Yes, I said again, but not out loud.

7

After school on Monday I raced up to Patrick's room. Patrick and Peggy were enjoying a quiet conversation. "Patrick!" I didn't mean to shout but it came out that way.

"Quietly, now, quietly," Peggy remonstrated.

"I *am* being quiet. Guess what, Patrick! I'm inviting Alex to come and visit you!"

Patrick looked startled. "Who?"

"Alex! The boy with the horse!"

Peggy broke in. "Now, Keely, I don't think you can just force this boy on . . . you need to be diplomatic."

"I'm completely diplomatic. More than diplomatic."

"I don't think you should rush into this with a total stranger. There's such a thing as being sensitive to. . . . "

"I'm as sensitive as anything. And I'm not in a rush. He's not coming today. Don't worry. He's coming, um, Wednesday."

"Forget it," said Patrick.

"He hardly knows anybody except dumb Charlotte. He only moved into town a few months ago. He said he'd like to meet you."

"He did?" Patrick paused, but thought better of it. "I'll bet."

"It's true. He thinks the two of you would have a lot in common."

"Why? Is he paralysed?"

Peggy fixed the pillows under Patrick's head. "Now, now," she said. "Meeting the boy might turn out to be a good idea, after all. He might have some interesting things to talk about."

Patrick sighed defeat.

"Good, that's settled," I said. "He'll be here at . . . four-fifteen Wednesday." I was fixing things, I thought, making things better for Patrick. I was beginning to feel a little Keely-the-Connorish, high up on my silver stallion, and it felt good. Now all I had to do was get hold of Alex and talk him into coming.

He was nowhere to be found at Sunny View Acres. Charlotte, on the other hand, was there, larger than life. "Where's Alex?" I asked.

"Not here."

"When will he be back?"

"Why?" Charlotte wanted to know. I wouldn't tell her.

"Does he have a phone?"

She merely arched her eyebrows.

"Where does he live?"

Charlotte yanked at her socks which kept slipping down into her now not-so-white sandals. I gave in, finally, and told her about my plan to invite Alex over to meet Patrick.

"Don't worry about a thing," Charlotte said. "We'll be there."

"We?"

"I'm very good with cripples," she said, looking back towards her house with its ramps and boardwalks. "I've had experience."

Alex was pedalling his bike up the lane as I was going down it on my way home. I asked him to stop and, gathering together everything I knew about being charming, invited him to meet Patrick on Wednesday.

"Sorry, I can't make it," he said.

I stared at him in surprise. I was crushed. I looked down,

biting the side of my lip, and looked up at him again, right into his eyes, so he could tell the world would come to an end if he didn't change his mind and agree to come just this once. "Please?" I said quietly.

"Oh . . . well . . . ," Alex said, finally.

"Wednesday at four-fifteen," I shouted, running towards home before he could change his mind.

Wednesday at four-fifteen, Alex, his hair carefully parted, his ears sticking out, but not unpleasantly, and Charlotte, frothy in pale pink with puffed sleeves, stood awkwardly in Patrick's bedroom. Peggy excused herself and said she'd get a plate of cookies. "You're the hostess, Keely," she said meaningfully, looking at the glasses of ginger ale on Patrick's dresser. I handed them around. There was an uneasy silence.

"How's Ginger?" I asked Alex.

"Okay."

"Ginger is Alex's horse," I explained to Patrick.

"You've already told me that fifty times."

"You should see Alex ride."

"Why?"

"Well, I mean. . . ."

"What a lot of books you have!" Charlotte smiled at Patrick.

"What would you expect me to have? Horses?"

"No, I just . . . I mean, I don't like horses. I like reading."

"Bully for you," said Patrick.

Alex frowned at me. "You know what you do if you have a mean, biting horse?"

"What?"

"You steer clear of his teeth." There was another strained silence. We sipped our ginger ale.

I held Patrick's glass with the bent straw close to his mouth, but he turned his head slightly and kept his lips together. Alex, his back to Patrick, looked out the window. "Sure is a nice day out. Does he ever go outside?"

"Who?" I asked, surprised.

"Him," said Alex, motioning over his shoulder with his thumb.

"You mean Patrick? Of course not."

"Why not?"

I looked at Patrick, not knowing how to answer. Patrick looked perplexed, then hurt. No one had ever done this to him before, treated him as if he weren't there, or as if he were a thing.

"Because I have no desire to go out," Patrick said, tight-lipped.

"What about school?" Alex turned to look at him.

"I don't go."

"What will you do when you grow up?"

Patrick's eyes were very large now. His lip trembled. I could see that he would either burst into tears or come out with a hair-curling string of obscenities. I sat on the side of his bed, a barricade between him and the world of sticks and stones. We were brother and sister, making a stand. I was an extension of Patrick, his fist if necessary. We were still joined at the mind. We glared at Alex, daring him to attack.

Alex looked from me to Patrick, then back again. There was sadness in his face, a little-boy sadness, as if someone had promised him something and then taken it away. I chewed my lip, trying to think of something to say. I didn't feel that Alex was an enemy as much as I felt that Patrick was a victim. Maybe this doesn't make sense, but there I was, sitting on the fence, trying to be on both sides at once. Before I could say a thing, Alex said, "How was I supposed to know he'd rather lie in bed than go outside in a wheelchair." Alex stood very tall now, his face stony with something like pride or stubbornness.

"He hasn't got a wheelchair." The fight was back in my

voice in spite of my fence-sitting.

"Why not?" Alex looked around the room at the overflowing bookcase, the train set up in a corner, the Meccano crane with a real motor, toys of Patrick's childhood too dear to give away. "He's got everything else."

Patrick, his voice thick, spoke in his own defence. "Would you like to be pushed around outside like a baby in a buggy? There's such a thing as pride. Did you ever think of that?"

"Well, no, not exactly," Alex said.

"That's what I thought."

"But I think I'd go loony if I couldn't get outside once in a while. I'd make a choice. I'd say, so what if I'm like a kid in a buggy, at least I'm out."

"Easy for you to say," Patrick whispered.

Alex clenched and unclenched his fist. He looked from Patrick to me again. "Sorry I can't stay," he said through his teeth.

"But . . . ," I began. I didn't want it to end like this.

"I can find the front door." Alex strode from the room.

"Alex?" Charlotte called faintly after him. "Oh well, don't mind him," she said. "He gets crabby sometimes. My mother says we have to make allowances for him because his father was killed in the war."

Killed in the war! Mygosh, I'd forgotten that Laurence had told me that; I'd spent all my imagination on the horse. I wanted to run after him, call him back, tell him I was sorry about his father, sorry about the war, sorry about the way Patrick and I seemed to gang together. From Patrick's window I saw him turn out of our walk and head briskly towards Sunny View Acres. I called to him to wait. He broke into a run and was soon out of sight.

I hoped Charlotte would follow him, but no, she stayed to finish her ginger ale. She stayed until Peggy brought the cookies. She stayed to devour five of them and to walk around Patrick's room touching things and asking questions with obvious answers. Peggy looked at me with raised eyebrows.

"Alex had to leave," I explained.

Patrick had had his eyes closed for some time. "Perhaps Patrick's a little tired now," Peggy suggested to Charlotte.

"Oh, sure," she agreed obligingly. She said goodbye and promised Patrick she'd return before long.

"Whoopie," Patrick sighed.

After Charlotte had gone, I told Peggy about Alex's father being killed in the war. "I wish I could do something for him," I said.

Peggy said, "I don't suppose there's much you or anyone can do, except be kind and sympathetic."

"Sympathetic!" Patrick broke in. "How? He's bad-tempered and he's bad-mannered. I hope I never see him again."

"You weren't exactly Little Lord Fauntleroy yourself," I said.

Patrick blocked me out by closing his eyes again.

Peggy put Patrick's splints on. He had them not just for his feet, but for his wrists and hands too. He was lost to us now, locked away in his own world. She began to clear away the cookie plate and glasses, and I helped her, following her down to the kitchen. "He seems so . . . flat," I said to her. I meant more than flat, but I had trouble finding the words.

"Patrick?" Peggy began to wash glasses.

"Yes. I don't just mean frail." He didn't make much more impression on his bed than a paper doll. "He just lies there, long and narrow. Like something's missing." I stared at the dishtowel.

"Maybe you mean he lacks a third dimension."

"Third dimension. Maybe, but I mean in his life. His life lacks . . . dimension. That's it. He needs more than those four walls of his room. He needs to count for something." I turned Peggy around to look at me. "Know what I mean?"

"Dry," she said. I started drying. "I think I know what you mean," she said.

I stopped drying to think again. "What he needs is someone to say to him, if it hadn't been for you I . . . ."

"I what?" Peggy emptied the dishwater down the drain. "Dry," she said.

"I don't know what the rest of the sentence is supposed to be." I picked up a glass and stared at it. "All he seems to think about is his own nothingness. His personality is so different from before, when we used to make bets and take risks." Peggy took the glass and the dishtowel from me and began to dry the glasses. "You know what? I've failed him."

"You can't solve all the problems in the world, Keely."

"I'm not trying to. I'm just trying to solve one." I picked up the dishtowel, but the glasses had all been dried. What was the point of dreaming up a silver stallion if I couldn't even make it go? Might as well be on a merry-go-round for all the good I was to Patrick. I didn't say any of this to Peggy.

She took the dishtowel and hung it up. "Put the glasses away, Keely," she said.

"He needs something to look forward to." I had two glasses in my hands and was staring thoughtfully into the cupboard. "But wait, he *has* something to look forward to — the big surprise package. You'd think he'd be asking about it every day. I would. But Patrick never gives it a second thought."

Peggy put the glasses in the cupboard. "You're no great shakes in the kitchen, Keely, but when it comes to saving the world, I'll bet my money on you every time."

Besides the surprise package, there was the search for Peggy's dead soldier. Even though it teetered between fantasy and reality, it still had some power to drag Patrick back from the black pit of despair. Of course, I couldn't discuss this with Peggy. I said to her as she was on her way to open the door for my mother, who was coming in with two shopping bags, "I guess it's the impossibility factor."

"What is?" my mother asked, putting the shopping bags

on the kitchen table.

I was thinking about the reason why Patrick was intrigued, even a little, about finding Peggy's fiancé. I didn't explain this to Mother or Peggy. I just said, "Maybe it's okay to fail if what you're attempting is impossible anyway."

They both looked at me and then they looked at each other with raised eyebrows. I went back up to Patrick's room.

"The thing about Alex," I said, before Patrick could tell me to get out, "is that he's actually nice." Patrick was staring at the wall. "Sure, he teased me when I tried to pretend I knew how to ride, but he was decent after the horse kicked me."

"The horse kicked you?" He was looking at me now. I sat cross-legged on the end of his bed and told him all about it. "And Alex taught me what to do without showing off. So what if he's moody, he has a right to be."

"He thinks he's so superior," Patrick complained.

"Maybe, but it seems to me his feelings are easily hurt. He's a bit proud, I think."

"Stubborn."

"Strong-willed. It won't be easy to win him back."

"Who wants to?"

I knew now that I wanted to — and I wasn't getting boy-crazy like Ginny. I got off Patrick's bed and looked in the small mirror that sat on his dresser. "I'm going to change, Patrick."

"Into what?"

I ignored his question. "It's not enough to *say* you're mature, you have to *be* mature." I stared serenely at my reflection and gave myself a cool, lips-only smile. With the right costume, I thought, the right scenery. . . . My smile was becoming a grimace.

"If you plan to turn into a moron, you've done it."

"Just wait. When you see the new me, you'll be

impressed. Even Mother will. She'll confide in me and take me seriously. She'll see how responsible I can be." I pulled myself up tall and thought, but didn't say out loud, I'll impress Alex so he begins to see me as someone whose brother he'd really like to know. I raised a fist and headed for the door. "I will attack maturity!" I vowed.

I swept my hair back from my face with a barrette that evening, but no one seemed to notice. My hair kept straggling out in spite of my efforts. I compared myself to the teenagers in Eaton's catalogue and discovered that my clothes were pitiful. Navy-blue tunics with pleats and a belt! Half the other girls in my class wore tunics too, but that was no consolation. They at least wore blouses with their tunics. I had to wear Patrick's white shirts, which he now had no use for. I rummaged through my mother's chest of drawers to find a costume of devastating maturity, and came up with a blue angora sweater set. In a weak moment Mother agreed to let me wear it to school. After all, it was the day before Good Friday — the last day of school before the Easter holidays.

"Bathe," she insisted before handing it over. I scrubbed myself raw. "No careless accidents, no ink-spills, no leaning against things and no perspiring." I agreed to everything.

I draped my bangs, most of them, to one side with a plain barrette. The blue angora short-sleeved sweater, topped by the matching long-sleeved cardigan, was very chic. I thought I looked stunning, womanly. I would never slouch again. I went in to Patrick to test the impact of my "new look". I stood in the doorway, one hand on my hip and the other behind my head, waiting for him to make some crude remark — provided he even noticed me.

Patrick stared; his jaw dropped. He looked shyly away, then. He wouldn't meet my eyes. I wondered if it bothered him that I was growing up and he was just, well, growing long. I couldn't leave him in this mood. "Hey!" I said. "Don't look so glum, chum. It's me, Katharine Hepburn, in person."

After a moment he rallied. "Whew, what a relief! For a minute I thought you were from a Roy Rogers movie."

"You did? Yeah, yeah, I know. The horse." We seemed to be almost back on familiar territory.

"Hey, Trigger," he called as I was leaving his room, "you can see right through your skirt."

I was pushing the season by wearing a light summer skirt. To solve the transparency problem I grabbed a petticoat of Mother's, yanked it on and bunched it up at the waist so it wouldn't hang down below my skirt. I straightened the skirt in front of the mirror and thought I was as close as spit to a vision of loveliness. At Mother's insistence I threw on my blue blazer, even though the piping drooped off the lapel, spoiling the movie-queen image I was aiming at. I slung the strap of my book bag over my shoulder and set off for school. A new person.

At first I thought the day would live up to my expectations. Mr. Leach called me to the blackboard for problem-solving. Someone at the back of the class whistled — probably that Buddy Dolan. Normally I couldn't stand him, but today I was prepared to take a fresh look at him. I always used to wonder why boys whistled at girls, but now I knew why. It was because some girls were simply irresistible and boys just couldn't help whistling. It was in their natures. I stood at the blackboard, irresistibly solving the first problem. Someone else whistled and then a couple of girls giggled.

Jealous, probably.

Mr. Leach made an attempt to bring order into the ranks. There were more giggles, whisperings and a chortle, likely from that stupid Buddy Dolan. I hated him, and I'd hate him for the rest of my life. I was beginning to feel somewhat less than irresistible. I polished off the problem on the blackboard incorrectly, but not caring, and returned to my seat.

"You're slipping about a mile," whispered Ginny.

"So what?" I whispered back.

"You look like a screwball," was all she had time to say before Mr. Leach towered above us, rapping on Ginny's desk with the yardstick.

A screwball! I risked looking around at the whistlers. Dolt-faced pea-brains! The world was cruel.

Ginny lent me a safety pin at recess. "It may be true that clothes make the man," I told Ginny, "but it takes a heck of a lot more than clothes to make a woman."

"I don't get it," Ginny said.

It was after school when things really deteriorated. Sun warmed the early spring air. I stood on the unmarked but well-defined border between the girls' side and the boys' side of the schoolyard, my spring blazer flung carelessly over one shoulder, and watched the boys play baseball. I was waiting for Ginny, who had to stay in after school for something she probably didn't even do and it probably wasn't her fault anyway, and that Old Man Leach was a pain in the you-know-what. Everyone knew that. I was engrossed in the boys' game. In my mind *I* was up to bat. I socked that ball to the far end. I made it to first, to second. At third I knew it would be a race. I slid home to thundering cheers and thumps on the back. Next I was on the other side, pitching against that so-called Romeo, Buddy Dolan. I wound up for a fast-ball, noting fear in his big blue eyes and a trembling in his muscle-bound arms. I had him nailed.

The ball, the real ball, sailed through the air. Dropping my jacket, I ran for it, never taking my eyes off it. I'd have caught it if the outfielder, running backwards for it, hadn't knocked me flying and then fallen on top of me, crushing me into the spongy schoolyard earth.

I didn't hang around any longer waiting for Ginny. I'd see

her at home; we had a full ten days of holiday ahead of us. I dragged on home, slouching along, hair in my eyes, my book bag on my back like a knapsack, boy-style. I didn't care. I had to think up a plausible story to explain the mess of Mother's sweaters. What was so great about a sweater set anyway? Just clothes. You have to cover yourself with something. Up ahead a little way, I noticed some kids fooling around, and one kid yelling blue murder. When I got closer I realized that two boys had a third one flattened on the ground. I knew the boy on the ground — Hartley Hodge, my lifelong enemy.

I don't know what got into me. It wasn't really the sort of thing I was famous for, but I did it anyway. "Scram, you kids!" I yelled fiercely. "Two against one's no fair."

The boys looked at me, cautiously, I thought, maybe because I was bigger than they were. And dirtier.

"Go on! Beat it! Why don't you pick on somebody your own size?" I threatened one of them with a closed fist.

They beat it. I dusted off my hands, gave the confused Hartley a superior glance and marched off down the street. Small potatoes, I thought, but all in a day's work. Keely the Connor rides again!

I took the long way home through downtown Channing. I needed time to rehearse a story about the sweaters. I turned onto Duffel Street. Across from the post office, Laurence Saunders was locking the door of Quinlan's Bakery. (He had bought the name too.) "How's Miss Doyle getting along?" he called.

"Who?"

"Nurse Doyle."

"Oh, Peggy. Fine," I replied. I would have asked why he wanted to know, but I had other things on my mind.

"Give my regards to her, and to your brother." Laurence tipped his hat and turned the corner.

I passed the post office and, when I got far enough along,

looked back and up at the town clock on top. It was twenty to six. I was late. They'd kill me. Oh well, I was a dead duck anyway.

I looked in the windows of John Rollins' drugstore. A display of spring cold remedies was arranged geometrically beside a small pyramid of boxes of baby soap. There were rolls of bandage and bottles of antiseptic. There were thermometers in cases and headache tablets in bottles and a warning about measles. The store was closed. Everything was closed. The street was deserted. I passed the newspaper office and the office of Ramage and Dewart, Barristers. I stood in front of the window of Nooke's Drygoods, where amid a neat assortment of children's socks and underwear and women's hosiery were arranged bolts of cloth. "For that new Easter outfit," a sign read. I moved along towards the bank at the corner.

Near the corner I noticed a man wearing a khaki coat, looking up the street one way and then down. He turned the corner hesitantly and then came back. He looked lost. Where his right arm should have been, the sleeve of his coat was pinned to his shoulder. I caught up to him. "Are you lost?" I asked.

The soldier turned his head away from me, but admitted he was lost. He was looking for the veterans' home. He had gone for a walk and had got himself turned around.

"Straight ahead two blocks, left for one and then right two blocks to the edge of town. I'm going that way myself."

"Thanks," he said, and set off ahead of me. I watched him through the hair in my eyes. I looked down at my scruffy clothes and shrugged. I must have looked pretty bad. I guessed he didn't want to be seen with a bum. I walked behind him at a discreet distance and noticed that he was tall. Extremely tall. Mentally I calculated his height in comparison to my own. Over six feet, well over six feet. I quickened my pace. Turning left he hesitated again, looking east, then west. I was behind him now.

"Left one block and then right," I said. The man ignored me. Curiosity shoved me forward. "Just move in?" I asked.

"Yes," he said, turning his head away. I tried to get a little ahead of him to look at his face but he turned his face further and stepped briskly forward. At the next corner he paused again, confused. He seemed unable to remember my directions.

"Right turn," I said, and the man wheeled right as if on parade. "My name is Keely Connor," I said brightly. He said nothing. I hardly ever gave up on something like this. "What's your name?" I asked, as politely as the situation allowed.

He didn't answer for a moment, and then he said, "I guess it's Joe."

"You guess?" The man walked on, face averted. "Don't you know for sure?" I couldn't understand this. How could he not know his name? We had reached our house.

"I can't remember." The man paused when I stopped, about to turn up our walk. He seemed confused again.

"You go that way, Joe. Just a little farther along."

He turned towards me now to see which way I was pointing. The right side of his face was badly scarred. He had a patch over his eye. I looked at my feet and swallowed hard. I looked up into his one eye and pointed along the road. "Just down there, Joe. There's your lane." I said it pretty softly.

"Thanks," he said. He walked on down the road, towards the setting sun, tall and lanky. I watched him turn safely up the lane and then headed up our walk. On the front veranda stood the remains of a large packing case. It had been pried open and the contents removed.

At last. Patrick's fortune was coming true. I ran inside.

CHAPTER

8

No one noticed my disarray when I walked in. Patrick was sitting in the front hall in a wheeled contraption with a built-up back and headrest like something on a dentist's chair. A tray was attached to it in front of his chest. Swivel rods projected up from the sides and held slings like flags at half-mast. The wheelchair, I later discovered, had been ordered made-to-measure, and purchased by Mrs. Fisk and the other ladies of the Hospital Auxiliary. This was the secret. More important than that, though, it fulfilled all Peggy's predictions of a large surprise that could make an impact on Patrick's life. I stood there, amazed. "It's the best invention in the world," I said to Patrick.

Patrick's mouth looked zippered shut. He glared straight ahead through a furious slit of eyelashes.

"Dinner's ready! Come and sit down, everyone." My mother's voice rang hollow with forced gaiety. Peggy placed Patrick's arms in the slings. He was powerless to resist. "With practice," she said, "you'll soon be able to feed yourself, Patrick." Patrick said nothing.

"And to use a pencil," said Father. "You'll be able to do some schoolwork. Mr. Leach has offered to come in the evenings to start you off."

"Old Man Leach!" muttered Patrick. "What would he

know? He only teaches grade eight. I'm supposed to be in high school."

"It would be a start, Patrick," Father said.

Patrick clamped his mouth shut and maintained a stony silence. Peggy held a forkful of green beans near his lips but he refused to open them.

You could almost choke on the tension, it was so thick. Father looked grim, Peggy seemed at her wit's end, Mother was fluttering, trying to smooth things over . . . until she took a close look at me. "What on earth!" she said.

I have to admit I cowered slightly.

"What happened to you?"

"It wasn't really my fault."

"Look at my sweaters! They're ruined!" Mother's voice had taken on her famous last-straw quality. Even Patrick was tempted to look at me.

"There was this fly-ball. . . ."

"You played baseball wearing my angora sweater set!"

"I didn't mean to."

"Keely, you are just the limit! You haven't a shred of responsibility."

Watching me squirm, Patrick opened his mouth for a bit of food in spite of himself. He lowered his head and slid his sling-encased arm and hand towards his chin to wipe away a crumb. Peggy held her breath but kept quiet. My eyes met Mother's again, hoping she'd get excited about Patrick and forget about me. It didn't happen.

"What am I going to do with you, Keely?"

Ginny's mother could have invented a drastic punishment or two. I was glad I wasn't Ginny.

"Perhaps, young lady, you can come up with an appropriate penalty." Mother glared. I looked down at the tablecloth and thought about jailbirds and what if I was handed a stiff sentence for something I hadn't meant to do. The actual crime took second place now as I saw myself with prison pallor, wasting in a dungeon. "Bread and water, I guess."

My father cleared his throat.

"Iron bars on my windows," I said cheerfully. I was really getting into the spirit of it and was going to say striped pyjamas next, with a number on the front. I looked up in time to see Patrick get another bite into him. He was looking at me with interest.

"That will do, Keely," Father said sternly.

"After dinner," Mother commanded, "you will wash those sweaters carefully in cold water, and at the same time I want you to think long and hard about becoming a mature and responsible young lady. You're nearly thirteen. Don't you think it's high time?"

"Yes." Easy enough to agree. Hard to make it happen. At least she hadn't threatened to cut off my allowance. That would have been a punishment worse than jail, with my own horse becoming reality nickel by nickel.

Dinner was soon over. Patrick asked to be taken back upstairs. I slaved over a sudsy bathroom sink full of muddy sweaters. I had to call down a couple of times to ask how much soap to use and how many rinses to give them. When Mother called up to say, "And roll them in a towel, don't wring them out," and I called back, "Too late, I already did," her last-straw voice went up a decibel. It was more like a blowing-her-stack tone of voice. Peggy came along then and said, "Don't worry, I think I can fluff them out." So I left her to it and went to see if Patrick was any happier about his chair.

"Isn't it gorgeous?" I said to him.

"It stinks."

"But now you can start living."

"Sure, living like a freak."

"Oh, Patrick," I sighed. I wanted to yell at him. I think I was beginning to understand Mother's last-straw attitude.

I had been looking forward to the Easter holidays. There

were several things I wanted to do without school getting in the way, and I went into Patrick's room to list them for him. I thought he might be interested. "First of all, I want to find out what I can about the tall, forgetful soldier." I had told Patrick about him, but he hadn't shown much interest.

"Why?" he asked dully.

"He could be Peggy's fiancé and not know it."

"Hardly."

"And then there's Alex."

"What about him?"

"He'll probably spend the holidays working at Sunny View Acres. That's what Laurence Saunders said. Maybe I can get him to give me more riding lessons." I glanced at Patrick to see how that struck him. He was staring vacantly at the wall. I danced back and forth within his line of vision but he didn't notice. "And I'm going to invite him back again to be your friend."

Patrick's eyes came alive. "Don't bother."

"Why not?"

"He doesn't like me. I could tell when he came that time, he looks down on me. He thinks I should be struggling to be something I never can be. A real person."

"But you are a real person."

"No I'm not. I'm a stick-doll with a brain."

I tried to argue with him, to point out that his brain was what made him real, but he locked me out as he usually did by closing his eyes and refusing to talk.

There was a church service on Good Friday. After it, I hauled a collapsible canvas deck-chair up from down cellar. I set it up on the front veranda, complete with the wooden-slatted footrest which hooks onto the front and turns the whole thing into a death-trap if you put pressure in the wrong place. Although it was still early April, it was warm and the chair made me believe that warmer days were not far off. I glimpsed Alex biking along Fairly Street heading for

Sunny View Acres. I would make him number one on my Easter list of things to fix. I leaned out over the veranda railing and waved at him but he didn't wave back. Possibly he hadn't seen me.

On Saturday, the day before Easter, Mother asked me to check the garden for rhubarb. Its little pinkish-red knobs were just poking through the earth. Through the fence high up in the pasture I could see Alex against a cloud-patched sky, leading Ginger out to fraternize with Lola and Bill. I called to him but he didn't answer. He probably hadn't heard. I watched as he walked out of sight down the other side of the slope. The clouds closed in, threatening a gloomy day. I had to get Alex to notice me. But how?

Ginny! That was how. She was good at attracting boys. The clouds broke and the sun beat down as I crossed the street to call on her. It made me feel warm and lucky. She came outside and sat on her front steps with me.

"Remember that boy Alex I told you about?" I was leaning back with my elbows resting on the step above. Across the street at our place the forsythia bush was coming into bloom.

"The guy with the horse? What about him?"

The sun beamed directly on the yellow forsythia, making me think of rainbows and pots of gold. "I want you to do me a favour." The scuddy clouds grew together again but it was ages before the bush lost its halo. I looked at Ginny to see if she had noticed, but she was flicking chipped paint off the steps with her thumbnail. I told her the bare bones of my plot to get back into Alex's good graces. She didn't commit herself immediately. "What does he look like?" she asked.

"Oh, well." I had to think. "Average, I guess." Ginny didn't seem very impressed. I glanced at her, narrowing my eyes. I had to use strategy. "He's quite tall, really. Very athletic. Blond hair (I couldn't actually make him up), I mean, fair hair. Magnetic eyes." I had read that once in a magazine story. Anyway, I couldn't remember the colour of Alex's eyes. Ginny was definitely taking an interest.

Mrs. Dickson opened the front door. "Ginny! Is your suitcase ready? Don't dawdle, now. We haven't got all day." Ginny jumped up. Her mother closed the door.

"Where are you going?"

"To my grandmother's."

"When will you be back?"

"Not till the end of the holiday."

"But," I said, "what about Alex?"

"Ginny!" Ginny's mother rapped sharply on the window. Ginny jumped again. "Coming," she called.

To me she said, "Keep an eye on him for me. I'll move in for the kill when I get back." She went inside. I kept on sitting there with my head in my hands, and my elbows on my knees. I began thinking unkind thoughts about Ginny, about Ginny's mother and even about Ginny's grandmother. The Easter holidays were going to be a fizzle. No doubt about it.

I ambled home kicking stones, drooping along, thinking about how things never turn out the way you hope they will. I glanced down the street towards the sign for Sunny View Acres. Gosh! I brightened a little. Old Charlotte might be pretty lonely all holidays. I set out to pay her a visit, keeping a sharp eye out for both Alex and the tall soldier. I found no one except Charlotte's brother, Hartley, who took one look at my purposeful strides and ran inside yelling, "Ma!" Mrs. Hodge said Charlotte was outside somewhere, possibly in the barn with the barn cat's new litter of kittens.

I went looking for Charlotte in a roundabout way. I searched the faces of the veterans sitting on the porch, but Joe, the tall man, wasn't among them. I checked the stable and climbed a fence for a better view of the pasture, but I didn't see Alex. I went back towards the barn *knowing* I would find Charlotte, but got waylaid by a glimpse of the old breadwagon left behind by Laurence in the driveshed. It looked a little faded, a little tired, but still in good order. It must have been sold along with the farm and horses. I climbed onto the bench seat and thought about Bill, the old horse, and how dismal he must be in his retirement with only mean Lola and young Ginger to knock around with. What if I hitched Bill up to the breadwagon and drove down the lane and along Fairly Street. If he was looking through his bedroom window, Patrick would get a jolt. And what if I called up to him and said, "Hey, Patrick! Want a ride?" And he said, "Sure." No reason he couldn't. If he could sit strapped into a wheelchair, he could sit strapped into a breadwagon. Couldn't he?

"What are you doing here?" Charlotte, from the wide arched door of the shed, looked at me as if I had criminal tendencies.

"Looking for someone," I said sweetly.

"Who?" She moved closer, the better to interrogate me.

Should I say Joe, the tall, scarred soldier? No. I wasn't prepared to share the quest for Peggy's dead soldier with somebody like Charlotte. She wouldn't look at it the right way. Should I say Alex? No again. Charlotte seemed to think she owned Alex. So I said, "You." I jumped down from the breadwagon, almost landing on her.

Charlotte looked first startled, then flattered. "I guess I should have figured that. Who else would you be looking for at our place?"

I shrugged. In the distance I could hear hammering. "What's the racket?"

"Alex is helping my father fix the barn roof."

"Let's go watch."

"Let's play Chinese checkers."

I made a face, but then noticed Charlotte beginning to look let down. "After," I said. "Promise."

"Oh, all right." We headed towards the barn, where we found Alex on the roof with Mr. Hodge hammering nails. Mr.

Hodge glanced at the clouds and hammered a little faster.

"Hi," I called over the din.

Charlotte's father looked surprised. "Hi there," he said. Alex just kept on pounding.

I kept looking up at him through my bangs, wondering what the magic formula was for attracting a boy's attention. If only I'd stuck the barrette in my hair! I looked at Charlotte, noting the big, floppy bow adorning one side of her head. Charlotte smiled back at me, showing to advantage her cute dimples. I felt like gagging. I looked up again at Alex and frowned. What was I, all of a sudden? Invisible?

Charlotte said, "Come on and see the new kittens." Dragging my heels, I followed her into the barn. "This one," Charlotte said, picking up the fattest one, "is mine." It was a beauty with yellow and orange markings. A marmalade cat.

I stroked it. "What are you going to call it?"

"Call it?" Charlotte looked as though naming a cat was a brand-new concept. "Puss, I guess," she said.

"Puss! That's not very original."

"That's what we called our other cat that we had a long time ago in Ottawa."

I shook my head. "What's the mother's name?"

"Puss. She came with the farm so we called her Puss."

Names ran through my mind. I liked distinguished names, memorable names. Winston Churchill, I thought. Dale Evans. "I know." I took the little orange cat. "Call it Patrick. Patrick Marmalade."

Charlotte wrinkled her nose. "It's kind of long," was all she said. She dragged me away from the barn towards the house. "Time for Chinese checkers."

I suggested we take Patrick Marmalade inside with us.

"I'm not allowed yet. It might bother the men. This one loony guy is afraid of cats. But he might be going soon, so maybe then."

I tried a long shot. "Who? Joe?"

Charlotte looked at me, astounded. "How did you know?"

I half-closed my eyes and smiled mysteriously. "I have my ways and means." No reason I couldn't pump Charlotte, as long as I was being forced into playing dumb games. "Why is Joe going soon?"

"He keeps getting lost. We're afraid something might happen to him. Anyway, my mother thinks he should go see a doctor. She doesn't like the look of him."

"It's not his fault. He can't help how he looks."

"No, she thinks he's coming down with something. That's what you say if you think someone is coming down with something — 'I don't like the look of you.'"

"Oh." I could imagine Charlotte saying it years down the road, as a grown-up lady. I could imagine Charlotte's children saying it. And Charlotte's grandchildren. A long line of frizzy, dimpled, cute-looking people muttering, "I don't like the look of you."

I got back to my detective work while Charlotte set up the game on the kitchen table. "What's Joe's last name?"

"Nobody knows. He was found over there in Italy or someplace with no identification and no memory. At the hospital they thought he might remember something living with us as part of a family. But it hasn't worked."

I kept thinking about Joe, and Charlotte kept beating me at Chinese checkers. I began to think logically. Two possibilities presented themselves. Either Joe was Peggy's dead soldier, or he wasn't. It all seemed so simple, boiled down like that. There was only one way to find out — get Joe and Peggy face to face. Yes.

"Well-l-l," I said politely, "fun as all this is, I've got to go now." I had to tell Patrick about my plan.

"You're just a sore loser."

"Don't be silly. I love losing."

"Come back tomorrow and we'll play Crokinole."

I turned down my mouth. "I hate Crokinole."

"Well, what game do you like, for goodness sake?"

"Spit."

Charlotte managed to wrinkle her nose and her upper lip and raise her eyebrows, all at the same time. I waved a quick goodbye and took off down the lane. Let it rain. Let it shine. At least I had the start of a plan.

"I wish I could sock you right in the jaw!"

I was just opening the front door.

"Patrick!" Peggy said. "You wouldn't hit a lady."

"I didn't say I would. I said I wished I could. I hate it when you torture me like this."

I came inside to find Peggy strapping Patrick into his hated chair. I had run all the way from Charlotte's to tell him my plan, and I was out of breath.

Patrick looked at me and looked away. "I wish I could sock everybody in the jaw." I stood there trying not to huff and puff, trying not to look as if I had been outside doing things. "I wish I could spontaneously combust," he said.

"Spontaneously what?"

"I wish I could will myself blown to bits." He closed his eyes. He was pale as death.

I slumped into a chair. Another bad day. I would have to get his attention somehow. I would have to get him back into my world before I could interest him in my newest plot.

"Think of the mess," I sighed. Patrick didn't respond.

"Be careful what you wish for," Peggy said. "Your wishes might come true."

Patrick opened his eyes and glared at her. "Sure," he said, "just like fortunes. Just like this chair. It wasn't a present for me, after all. It was for you, so you could torture me, make a freak of me. And the other part of the fortune, that trip I'm supposed to take. That really came true, didn't it! I get to go from the dining-room to the living-room. Big, hairy deal. Excuse me while I pack my bag." He sank back against his headrest and shut out both of us.

We looked at each other. Peggy pressed her lips together and shook her head sadly. I drew my eyebrows together and came up with an idea. "I bet . . . you'd be afraid to go outside."

Patrick ignored me.

"I dare you to go outside."

Patrick threw me a glance, finally. "That game is over, Keely. Dead men don't take dares."

"So who's dead? Come on, Peggy, we're taking him outside onto the veranda!"

"Oh, now, Keely," Peggy cautioned.

Too late. I grabbed the afghan from the living-room couch and wrapped it around Patrick, tucking it in around his shoulders. Patrick stared at me as if I'd gone crazy. I got behind the chair and pushed it towards the front door.

"Oh no you don't!" yelled Patrick.

"Open the door, Peggy," I ordered.

Cautiously, Peggy opened the door. "Keely, be careful."

"I hate this!" Patrick yelled. "Stop it! I don't want to be on the veranda."

Mother came running from the kitchen. "Oh dear," she said, at a loss for anything more authoritative.

"Get away from me! I'll kill you for this! I hate you!" Patrick's lungs were amazingly strong.

I bumped him over the doorsill and along the front veranda towards a patch of sunlight glinting through the parted clouds. Patrick let loose a string of swear-words that impressed even me, but I kept on pushing him.

"Patrick!" Mother was shocked. "Think of the neighbours! I hope to heavens Mrs. Dickson can't. . . . "

Peggy hovered.

Suddenly Patrick was bathed in spring sunshine. I stopped the chair and turned it so the sun shone directly on his face. He was still swearing, but not as imaginatively.

"I'll get his pills," Mother said.

"Maybe you shouldn't," Peggy suggested. "They could be harmful if we give them too often. He may calm down on his own."

Patrick stopped, finally, out of breath. He panted through his open mouth. He squinted against the blinding sunlight and turned his head slightly. Still breathing hard, he whispered, "I can feel it."

"What?" I bent closer.

"I can feel the sun." He opened his eyes.

9

I thought getting Patrick outside onto the veranda was like leaping a major hurdle, that all we had to do was go on to the next. That wasn't how it worked out. Each time I tried to repeat the trek to the veranda, Patrick rebelled. It seemed to me that he was following some ritual, rebelling for the sake of rebelling, not because he genuinely wanted to stay indoors. It was a bid for power. I finally saw the light and pretended I couldn't care less whether he stayed in or went out. Once he had made his point, he had a choice. He chose to go out. I began to feel as though one small part of one large problem had been fixed.

We sat on the veranda, our faces to the sun, the spring breeze gently lifting our hair. I told Patrick about the latest dead-soldier developments. Somehow, outside, the scheme didn't sound so far-fetched. Patrick, of course, was skeptical. "The chances of this guy being Peggy's fiancé are one in a million." The ice truck went by dripping water, spilling sawdust. We watched it out of sight.

"I'm willing to go along with the odds," I said. I stretched out on the deck-chair.

"Anyway," he continued, "even if he was the one, he wouldn't remember being engaged to Peggy if he can't remember his own name." A robin trailing a long piece of dead grass from its beak flew onto the veranda railing and eyed us.

"But that's the sort of thing that would jog his memory, don't you see?" The robin flew away, probably deciding the veranda was a poor nesting risk.

"Sure, in some corny movie, but not in real life, Keel. Come down to earth."

"You never know. I'm a very romantic person, and I'm not giving up."

"You're a very lame-brained person, you mean, which would explain why you're not giving up."

Once while we were on the veranda Joe walked past, accompanied by another veteran. "He's not allowed to walk out alone in case he gets lost," I explained. The next morning, from our usual spot, we saw Joe pushing a man in a wheelchair. Patrick stared after them until they were out of sight. We sat out again in the afternoon and I started making up what-if stories about Joe for Patrick's benefit.

"What if we managed to get Peggy and Joe together?"

"Oh, well." Patrick decided to play the game. "If it's just on the what-if level, then I guess anything could happen. Peggy would take one look at him and scream, 'Derek!' "

"Derek? Is that her fiancé's name?"

"I don't know. This is only what-if, remember? Anyway, it's a pretty good romantic name. And then Peggy would fall into a swoon and faint dead away."

"And then," I added, "Derek would shake his head hard as if he had water in his ears and stare all around and say, 'Wh-wh-where am I?' "

"And then. . . ." Patrick was as carried away now as I was.

"Yoo-hoo," rang out a cheery voice. We looked out to the street. Charlotte was standing there beside Joe. Patrick and I glanced at each other out of the corners of our eyes.

"Why don't you bring Joe up to meet Patrick," I invited.

"Would Joe like that?" Charlotte sounded as though she

were talking to an infant.

"Sure," he said. Charlotte led the way up the veranda steps and turned to make sure Joe was following. He tried to keep the scarred side of his face turned away.

"Hi there, Joe. I'm Patrick." This was the first time Patrick had shown any friendliness to anyone since his illness.

Before Joe could answer, he sneezed. "Sorry," he said. He shook out a handkerchief, blew his nose and put the handkerchief back in his pocket. "How're you doin'?" he said, and gave Patrick's limp hand a light squeeze. He nodded at me, not recognizing me. He began to cough then, and couldn't seem to stop.

"Cover your mouth when you cough, Joe," Charlotte said.

"Sure," he said and immediately forgot.

"I wonder what Peggy's doing?" I looked meaningfully at Patrick. "Maybe she'd like to come out and meet Joe."

"Keely," Patrick said, "this is real life now, remember?"

But I was already inside calling Peggy. I returned and told everyone she'd be right out. "So," I said, making conversation, "where are you heading for, or are you coming back from downtown?" Peggy opened the door and stood there a moment to put her sweater around her shoulders.

"We're just coming back from the doctor's," Charlotte said.

Peggy came out onto the veranda. Patrick and I both studied her face, not listening to Charlotte rattle on. I tried to calculate which way Peggy might fall when she fainted, and hoped either Charlotte or I would be close enough to catch her.

"The doctor thinks," Charlotte continued, "Joe might have the measles."

Peggy gasped. Her face went chalk-white. We watched her reaction, gaping, waiting for her to scream "Derek!" or some other romantic name.

"Measles!" she yelped. "Measles, and you brought him

here?" She glared at Charlotte. Joe coughed gently, without covering his mouth.

"I'm sorry," Charlotte murmured.

"Sorry," Joe said.

Peggy opened her mouth and closed it. "Well," she spluttered. "Well." She looked at Joe's scarred face, his empty sleeve. She seemed to soften. The colour returned to her face. "Perhaps the gentleman should go home to bed now. He doesn't look well."

Joe smiled at her. "Sure," he said.

Crestfallen, Charlotte led Joe down the steps. "The doctor didn't say for sure he *had* the measles. He hasn't any spots. He said, time will tell." Charlotte seemed close to tears. She yanked at the backs of her socks. Farm life had done her white shoes no good at all. They looked as forlorn as Charlotte herself.

Peggy said, "It's all right, dear. Don't be upset. It's just that measles are terribly contagious and people get very sick with them."

Charlotte brightened. "Oh, don't worry, I've already had them."

Peggy's face looked grim again. "That's all very well for you, dear, but not everyone may have been so lucky."

Charlotte waved a cheery goodbye. Peggy took the back of Patrick's wheelchair and pushed it inside. I said, "We've had them too, Peggy. Don't worry."

"*You've* had them," Peggy said, "I've looked at both your medical files."

"Hasn't Patrick?"

"No," said Peggy.

"Oh, big deal," said Patrick. "Fuss, fuss, fuss. Is that all women know how to do? I talked to the guy for a total of five minutes. I'm sure I'm going to catch his stupid measles." Peggy didn't say anything. "Anyway, sounds like he just has a cold. Adults don't get measles."

Peggy continued to say nothing.

"Peggy," I began slowly, "didn't you take a good look at Joe?"

"Who?"

"The man."

"Not particularly."

"Didn't he look familiar? I mean, on his unscarred side?"

"Never laid eyes on him in my life."

I rolled my eyes at Patrick. He looked wryly back. "I keep telling you, Keel, old girl, this is real life. Not the movies." Peggy looked at us with one raised eyebrow and shook her head very slowly.

Patrick seemed all right after his exposure to Joe. I pointed this out early next day to Peggy and my parents. Father was on his way to the court-house. He said, "It's going around, I hear. The Crown attorney's daughter is running a high fever. Had to have the doctor twice. Keep a close eye on that lad." Concern showed in the lines of his face as he left.

Mother worriedly shook her head. "I don't see how Patrick could withstand a bout with measles at this stage. He's still so delicate."

"He's fine," I said.

"Keely, dear," Peggy said, "it doesn't show up right away. It takes days. Let's just keep our fingers crossed."

Later in the day Mrs. Hodge phoned to say the doctor was pretty sure Joe just had a bad cold. Mr. Hodge was taking him back to the veterans' hospital in Toronto. It was safer for him there, with his bad memory.

I relayed the news to Patrick in his room. "Now what'll we do? We'll have to figure out a whole new strategy."

"Give it up," said Patrick. "It's a waste of time."

"I never give up." I sat there plotting.

Peggy found us both staring at the wall. "Charlotte phoned, Keely. She wondered if you wanted to go over to play Crokinole."

"N.O."

"And she said something about that Alex boy's horse. She knows you'd like to ride it again."

"Really?" I looked at Patrick. "Nah, I don't feel like it."

Patrick snorted. "Since when? Go on, Keely. I'm sick of the stupid game we're playing here."

I stayed put.

"Go!"

I frowned. "Why do you want me to go?"

"'Cause maybe you'll fall off the horse on your head and get some sense knocked into you."

"All right for you! I will go." I lifted my chin and strode out.

Charlotte was waiting for me at the top of the lane. When I suggested we skip the game and just ride Alex's horse, she scowled and crossed her arms, but I didn't give in. She sighed. "We could play with the barn kittens." I shook my head and pointed my thumb towards the high pasture. When Charlotte said she had some Lana Turner and Betty Grable cut-outs she'd let me play with, I said, "Blech!" and turned as if I were heading for home.

"Oh, all right!" Charlotte ran after me. "We can do whatever you want."

I stopped to see if there was a catch. "How come?"

"If you go home, my mother will make me play with Hartley."

I thought about that. I decided I could afford to do old Charlotte a favour. "Okay, I'll stay."

We saw Alex carrying old boards from what had once been a hen-house to the driveshed, where he stacked them against the wall near the breadwagon. The hen-house was to be restored. Alex nodded silently when I greeted him, and kept on working. When I inquired after the health of his horse, he only grunted something incoherent.

"Does he hate me, or something?" I asked Charlotte when he was out of earshot.

"Probably."

"Why?"

She gave me a long, head-to-toe appraisal, as though she could think of dozens of reasons, but all she said was, "He thinks you and your brother are stuck-up."

"Stuck-up! Patrick and I are both very humble and very kind-hearted human beings."

"Like heck! Patrick says mean things and you let him. You even agree with him. You spoil him and protect him too much and make everybody else feel left out."

"But. . . . "

"You made Alex feel awful when he said Patrick should go out in a wheelchair. You didn't stick up for him at all."

"But. . . . "

"And. . . ." Charlotte seemed unable to stop. "You make me feel awful, too."

"I do?"

"You didn't just come over to see me."

I looked down at the ground. What could I say?

"You came over to see Alex. Or see his horse, is more like it."

I said, "Well, not entirely. . . . "

"You don't like me. You never stand up for me."

"Gosh, Charlotte. . . . " I tried to imagine how a hero would get out of these accusations, but nothing came to mind. If Charlotte were drowning or something, I'd leap right in and rescue her, but. . . . I blurted out the first thing that came into my head. "I'm sorry," I said.

"I bet." Charlotte walked away from me, heading for the house. Just the way she walked along, her head up as if she couldn't care less, her floppy bow half untied, her shoes all scuffed and run down at the back, made me feel kind of sad. She reminded me of our Christmas tree just before we take it down, with its drooping branches and bits of old tinsel we forgot to remove.

"Hey, Charlotte," I called.

Charlotte stopped. "What?" she asked, without turning around.

"I'll play you a game of Crokinole."

"You will?" She turned, wary.

"Sure, I'll play anything." I walked along beside her towards the house and didn't even look back for Alex.

"Guess what," Charlotte said. "I'd rather play cut-outs. You see, with Betty Grable and Lana Turner we can pretend they're in a movie and. . . . "

"Be-t-t-y Gra-a-ble and L-a-n-a Tu-r-n-er!" I couldn't believe it. "You actually want me to cut out paper dolls?"

"They're all cut out. We just dress them in different styles."

"I think I'm going to be sick."

Charlotte stopped. "See," she said, "I knew it. You're not interested in me." She sighed heavily.

I gritted my teeth. This was not the kind of hero I had planned on turning out to be. Not what I wanted to be famous for. I sighed heavily too, and said, "Come on, let's play cut-outs."

"Goody!" said Charlotte, flashing her dimples.

"I have only one request," I said. "I get to change their names."

"To what?" Charlotte was wary again.

"To Dale Evans and Roy Rogers."

"That's stupid. How can you do that?"

"Easy." I strode fiercely ahead. From the corner of my eye I saw Alex come out of the driveshed. Charlotte caught up to me in the lane heading for the house. I needed to apologize to Alex, but not here, not in front of Charlotte. I had to choose the right time, the right setting.

"Hey, watch out, you guys!" Alex, behind us, on his way to the hen-house, cautioned us. When we turned to look at him he pointed straight ahead and a little to our right. A skunk waddled out of the long grass into the lane to meet us. He stopped not ten feet in front of us and waved his nose up and down. "Back up," Alex said, as quietly as he could and still make us hear.

"Oh, for heaven's sake," I said. "Who's afraid of a skunk?"

"I am," volunteered Charlotte. "Help," she said, looking at me. "What should we do?"

"Don't worry," I said calmly. "I'll look after this. Shoo!" I said to the skunk. The skunk held his ground.

Alex called, "Just back away slowly. Don't make any sudden movements." Charlotte began to back away towards Alex.

"There's nothing to get excited about," I said. "I'll hold him at bay until you make your getaway, Charlotte, and then I'll scare him off."

"Don't be stupid," Alex called. "You're going to get sprayed, Keely."

I looked at the two of them over my shoulder and shook my head. "Skunks are just as frightened of you as you are of them." To the skunk I said, "Scram!" and clapped my hands. Maybe I overdid it. The skunk was more than frightened. He was mad. He demonstrated this in the only way he knew how, I guess. Then he took off.

I admit that I howled. My eyes burned. I couldn't catch my breath. Skunk-gas took over the world.

Alex hooted. He was doubled over with laughter. He held his nose and pointed at me and danced a little jig. With owl eyes Charlotte looked from Alex to me and back. "Are you all right?" she asked me. I didn't answer.

I knew I had reached the depths, the absolute Grand Canyon, of embarrassment. All I could do now was rise above it. I stood very still, like a soldier at attention, blinking my eyes rapidly and taking short breaths. Alex stopped laughing and stared at me. Charlotte repeated her question. I waited until I had their full attention. "Yes," I said, "I'm just fine." I went on. "I would like to apologize, Alex, for anything I may have done to upset you when you came to visit Patrick. I didn't mean to insult you. I just want to say that Patrick and I still want you to be his friend. *If"* (I emphasized the if) "you would do us the favour." I put my chin in the air and marched towards home.

"Who would have believed it?" I heard Alex say. "Talk about style!"

"Thank you, Keely," Charlotte called. "Thank you for protecting me."

I didn't turn around. I gave a careless "think-nothing-of-it" wave of my hand and kept on walking. I was Keely the Connor, without a horse, so I just kept on walking home.

"Ooo-ow!" Mother poured another tin of tomato juice over me. "It stings like Billy-o." I was scrunched, fully dressed, into a washtub on the back stoop.

"Do you want to go back to school smelling like a skunk?"

"No!"

"Well then, close your eyes. I'm going to pour some over your head."

"Yow," I yowled.

As it turned out, I had no choice about taking my skunk-smell to school. In spite of the tomato juice I still reeked, and school would resume in three days. No matter how hard I tried to shove back the clock, the evil day ticked closer. No matter how often I bathed in bath salts, bubble bath, Ivory Snow, Bon Ami, Lifebuoy and baking soda, I still smelled unmistakably of skunk. These long and frequent solitary confinements in the bathtub gave me time to consider my predicament. Things like skunks didn't happen to most people. Never to Charlotte. Probably not even to Ginny. Sure, other people might have things happen to them, but they would be reasonable things like breaking a leg or getting kidnapped. Why, I wondered, did I get the skunks and everyone else get the romantic adventures?

It was probably because I didn't look right. Only beautiful things happen to beautiful people. If only I had curly hair, or a sophisticated arch to my eyebrows, or even a hint of a dimple or two. That's what I needed to keep the skunks away. I dried myself, surrounded myself with a haze of Yardley's Lily of the Valley dusting powder — and emerged smelling like a skunk.

Ginny, back from her grandmother's, met me outside her house on the first day of school. I had prepared her over the phone for a faint whiff of skunkiness, and she had promised to sit beside me no matter what.

"Holy liftin'!" she said from her front steps when I approached. She held her breath and puffed out her cheeks.

"You promised," I reminded her.

Ginny agreed that she had. "But I didn't promise not to hold my nose," she was quick to say.

By the time we had got through the Lord's Prayer and "God Save the King", and by the time we had pledged allegiance to the flag and to the King and Empire, and by the time Mr. Leach had got round to calling the roll, each student answering "present", the whole grade-eight class knew. Only Mr. Leach, our teacher and principal of the school, was still in the dark. "I hope there's not a skunk in the schoolyard," he said, looking out the window. The class was convulsed. Mr. Leach seemed to know all about adolescent students. He said that he knew it didn't take much to set us all laughing and that he was prepared to be tolerant. "I wonder if we might have some brave lad check outside for us. We wouldn't want to send the wee ones out for recess if there was a skunk prowling about." The class roared. Mr. Leach was determined not to crack down too hard the first day after a holiday. "Could we have a volunteer to look around?" The class did everything but roll in the aisles.

I stood up. "I'll volunteer."

"Oh," Mr. Leach said, "but perhaps a boy. . . ."

"I've had experience."

The class held its aching sides.

"Well. . . ." Mr. Leach was doubtful. "A brave girl? It's possible, I guess. Well, Keely, then," he said. "But if you see something, don't linger."

"No sir." I went outside. I walked around the school twice and went back in.

Mr. Leach put down his chalk. "Anything out there, Keely?" The class tried unsuccessfully to smother its giggles.

"'Fraid so, sir." The class stared with raised eyebrows. "A mother and four little ones."

"That's bad." Mr. Leach seemed to know about skunks too, and one of the things you never do is disturb a mother with babies. The class hovered between doubt and belief.

"They've found something to eat," I said, "and they won't clear out till they finish it. Not only that, they may hang around looking for more food." My story sounded authentic. The class looked puzzled.

"Well, that does it," Mr. Leach said. "I'll have to cancel recess." Groans from the class. Everybody looked daggers at me.

I looked back, thinking hard. "I've heard of skunks who've hung around for up to five hours just looking for food."

Mr. Leach sent a boy with a message to each teacher, advising that recess had been cancelled for the morning, along with an explanation and a promise that the teachers would be kept posted as to further developments.

Mr. Leach returned to the blackboard, but paused before writing — he must have been thinking about skunks. He paced back and forth like a general with troops under siege, surrounded by the enemy, no chance of getting out. We heard his stomach rumble. He moistened his lips — thinking, possibly, of the hot meal his wife would have ready for him at noon when he got home — if he got home. His stomach rumbled again. He coughed loudly, stealthily took a horehound cough lozenge from his pocket and popped it into his mouth. He stared sadly into his pocket. Rations must be running low.

Then Mr. Leach sat down at his desk and wrote a message to be delivered by a boy to each class. He read it out to us. Every pupil and every teacher should evacuate the building quickly, quietly and in single file through the boys' entrance (the skunks, I guess he figured, had taken up positions at the girls' entrance) and not return until next day. In the meantime he would do everything in his power to infiltrate, he coughed and changed the word, rid the schoolyard of the menace.

When he announced this plan to our class a cheer went up. He seemed to glow all over. "When you're in command," he said, "command." We cheered again.

"What did the babies look like?" Ginny wanted to know on the way home. "I bet they were cute."

"What babies?"

"The skunk babies, stupid."

"There weren't any skunk babies, stupid. I made it all up. Come on, let's run. We have the day off."

I started to run but Ginny just stood there with her mouth open. "Keely Connor! Boy, that's some nerve!"

"Come on!" I yelled, running sideways to see what was keeping her. Ginny caught up and we laughed our heads off. We laughed till we had to stop and cross our legs.

Ginny said, "Not even I would have gone that far, Keely."

"Yes, you would. If you had half the school laughing at you, you would. If you had half the school believing you threw yourself in the path of a skunk to save Charlotte Hodge, you would. That's the story she's telling everyone." We tore along the street and pounded up our front steps just as a distant cheery yoo-hoo reached our ears. We were inside like a shot, panting, leaning our backs against the door.

"What," said my mother, "is the meaning of this? Did the school burn down?"

I wished I could say yes. Instead I said, "Mr. Leach thought there were skunks in the schoolyard so he sent everyone home."

"My word!" said Mother. "We seem to be getting more than our share of skunks this spring." She continued on her way upstairs carrying a pile of freshly ironed and folded sheets. There were no further questions asked.

Ginny and I wandered into the living-room and there, his head pressed back against the headrest of his chair as if he were trying to be invisible, was Patrick. Ginny stopped in the doorway and bit her lip. Patrick stared, unblinking, straight ahead.

"Um," I said.

Ginny stepped hesitantly into the room. She had that stricken look she had had the day Patrick threw his fit and told her he hated her. But she pulled her face back together and looked directly at him. "Don't yell at me, Patrick. I have something to say that I've been thinking about for a long time."

Patrick blinked but didn't look at her.

"I've decided to become symbolic."

Now Patrick did look at her. "What?" he said.

"If you would think of me as symbolic, you wouldn't hate me. So, I'm symbolic."

There was a pause. Patrick and I looked at each other. I said, "It makes sense to me. I know what she means."

"It wouldn't make sense to most people," Patrick muttered.

I stared him in the eye. "I can tell that it makes sense to you. You know what she means."

Ginny stood quietly, looking from Patrick to me while we communicated in our own private way, as though she weren't even present. Patrick's eyes slid sideways but he didn't say anything.

Ginny started back through the door. "I better go. My mother always kills me when I don't go straight home."

"Ginny!" It was Patrick calling her.

She turned and looked at him, not smiling, not looking hopeful, not even looking angry.

"Right," Patrick said softly. "I know what you mean."

Ginny nodded and said, "See y' around." Then she left.

I could have hugged Ginny, but of course we never hug, because we think it's so affected. I even decided, generously, that if Ginny chose to save Patrick instead of me from the firing squad, well, heck, let her.

10

When Ginny left, I pushed Patrick's chair into the back parlour. Peggy had left him to his own devices while she went out to do a little shopping. The parlour, a cozy sitting-room, had a large window that looked out onto the back yard and the field beyond our fence. "You should move down here, Patrick. This would make a nice room for you."

"Why bother? My old room will do me until I die."

"Come on, don't talk like that."

Patrick gazed through the window. In the high pasture beyond the fence three horses munched new grass on the brow of the hill. The brilliant sky hung behind them like a backdrop. "Don't say anything to Ginny," he said, "but I don't think about things being symbolic much any more. Like heroes riding horses and all that."

"I do."

"Fine, go ahead. I've outgrown that sort of thing."

I sat on a chair beside him and stared into his face. "Don't be such a poop."

"Keely, do you mind backing off about six feet? You're a bit overpowering. Skunks really seem to follow you around, don't they? Do you think there's something symbolic in that?"

"Patrick!" I backed off, but not far.

"They even follow you to school."

"There were no skunks at school. Mr. Leach sent me out to check so I made it up."

"You mean you lied?"

"I didn't exactly lie." I got up and went to the window.

"What did you exactly do?"

I felt uncomfortably warm. "What is this, the third degree? I'm no baby, you know. I'll be thirteen next month. You're not my boss."

"No, I just wonder what your definition of a lie is."

"All right. All right. I lied. So what are you going to do, tell on me?" I turned and glared at him.

"That would be just about as immature as lying."

"Oh, drop dead!"

"I wish I could." His face drooped wearily.

"Patrick! That's just an expression. You can't wish yourself dead. It's wrong."

"I see. According to you it's okay to lie, but wrong to wish yourself out of everyone's hair. Think about it, Keely. I'm no good to anyone. It costs a lot to look after me. Some day you'll grow up and get married and move away. Our parents will get old. Some day they'll die. I've been thinking about these things for a long time. I'm not just saying it to get a rise out of you, and I wouldn't say it to anyone else, but that's how I feel."

"I'll look after you for the rest of my life, Patrick. I wouldn't get married even on a bet. We'll live here all our lives. No, wait." I pointed to the field beyond the window. "That's where we'll live. Just you and me and some horses." I leaned over his chair, but backed off when he flared his nostrils.

"Keely, grow up, for Pete's sake."

"Grow up! Obviously I'm more grown up than you are. At least I don't think about how to spontaneously combust or drop dead all the time."

"Keep your voice down, Keely."

"I mean, it's stupid. You can't hold a gun and point it at your head. You can't jump off a bridge. You can't plunge a dagger into your. . . . " I was in front of him now, pointing a finger at my head, thumping a daggerless fist into my heart.

"Keely, just shut up, will you?"

I shut up. Briefly. After a short pause I said, "You know, you could try a new kind of living. I mean, look at babies. Supposing we all start off as babies."

"We do."

"I know, but listen. See, we're all swimming around inside our mothers, no cares, no problems. Then, bang. All of a sudden we're born. Suddenly we're like a fish out of water. But we adapt, see? Slowly we learn to get along in the real world. And babies only have these little pea-brains to learn with. But look at you, you have this big, almost adult brain, so you should be able to figure out a new way for a fish to live out of water."

"Boy, you're a real Einstein, aren't you?" He gazed out the parlour window, not impressed by the vivid green or dazzling blue.

"A what?"

"Forget it." Patrick, silent, had that unfocused look. The window might as well have been a wall.

I saw a bad day coming up. Quickly I said, "Okay, I dare you. In fact, I double dare you." I stood in front of him.

His gaze drifted towards me. "To do what?"

"To think of a way to live. To find yourself a life."

Patrick closed his eyes. In a moment he opened them and glanced out the window. He said in a teasing tone, "Why don't you go outside? The skunks are lined up waiting for you. Hoping for an invite to your grand, ceremonial thirteenth birthday."

So he wasn't going to take the dare. I looked sadly out into bleakness.

Peggy came in then, still in her coat. She started telling us something about Laurence Saunders opening another bakery across town. We looked at her with polite but scant interest. "He drove me home from downtown," Peggy said. "Told me it was on his way, but I don't believe it really was. Peculiar man."

"Who?" I looked dully at her.

"Laurence Saun . . . what's the matter with you two?" Peggy put her parcels down while she slipped out of her coat.

"Nothing."

"I hear the school's been attacked by a herd of thundering skunks. I thought you'd be rejoicing."

"Who told you?"

"Ginny. She was on her way over here with a present for Patrick. She asked me to give it to you, Patrick."

"Why didn't she bring it herself?" I asked.

"No idea. Something about not wanting to press her luck." It was a long, thin package done up in tissue paper and tied at both ends with red string. "I'll open it for you, if you like," Peggy offered.

"Be my guest," Patrick said, with a studied lack of interest. She freed the object from its wrapper and held it towards him. He frowned. I started to form a question, but stopped. She put it down on his tray.

"What a useless thing that is!" Patrick scoffed. "Has Ginny lost all her marbles? What am I supposed to do with a charcoal pencil, eat it?"

"People do draw with their mouths, you know," I was quick to say.

"Sure, freaks," said Patrick.

Peggy said, "If we built it up somehow, made it fat enough for you to grasp, you could use it."

"No!"

Peggy continued. "Remember the old lumber we talked

about? This is what I meant. You have to sort through it and see what you can still use. You used to draw pictures of horses. Maybe you can again."

"No!" Patrick was working himself into a temper tantrum. Peggy turned away.

"You could at least try it," I said.

"Are you deaf or stupid or both? Can't you hear me saying no? I will *not* try it. No matter what kind of squiggly line I produced, you'd all ooh and aah over it as if it was a masterpiece, and I'd know you were lying. Go away! Leave me alone!"

What could we do? We left him alone.

The next day at school, Mr. Leach had to admit that he had been unsuccessful in rounding up the invisible skunk family. He stood near my desk and eyed me with suspicion. "You didn't tangle with those skunks, did you, Keely?"

"Well, sir, I have to admit I did get sprayed by a skunk."

"Hm!" Mr. Leach said. "I knew I should have sent a boy to investigate."

Ginny didn't ask me what Patrick thought of the charcoal pencil that day or even the next, but she kept looking at me with wide, questioning eyes. By Friday after school her curiosity was too much for her. "Well?" she asked. She had me cornered.

I couldn't hurt her feelings. "He's mulling the idea over, I think. He hasn't used it yet because he's been staying in bed the past few days. He got overtired." This was true. He had returned to his bed after his outburst and flatly refused to be taken out again. Peggy gave in, saying he did look tired.

Ginny seemed satisfied with the explanation. "The reason I gave it to him was because I said I'd try to think of some way of getting back his old personality. Now that I'm a symbolic friend, I thought I could get him interested in finding a way to make symbolic drawings of symbolic horses. Do you think it'll work?"

"It might. I hope so."

"I mean, speaking symbolically," she added.

"Ginny," I said, "you are getting close to becoming a symbolic bore."

We were walking home from school and making plans for Saturday. Ginny wanted me to go to the show with her to see a movie starring Gene Autry. I was tempted to part with some of my savings, because Gene Autry has a nice horse, but when Charlotte caught up to us we changed the subject. Charlotte interrupted. "I've got an idea. Let's all three go to the show tomorrow afternoon."

Ginny rolled her eyes at me and turned down the corners of her mouth. I mumbled, "Gosh, Charlotte, actually, you see, um. . . ." I glanced at Charlotte's hope-filled face. Ginny was waiting for me to make up an excuse. Charlotte began to get that doomed look in her eyes that I had seen before. I cleared my throat. "Actually, Charlotte. . . . " I screwed up my face, thinking hard. "That'd be dandy. We can all go." Ginny's mouth dropped and she scowled. "Okay, Gin?"

"Sure," Ginny said through tight lips. "Whatever you say, Joan of Arc."

Charlotte's scuffed shoes seemed to dance.

Alex whistled by on his bicycle, heading for Sunny View Acres. He called a "Hi!" over his shoulder. Ginny nudged me. "Is that the guy? Is that Alex?" she mouthed. I nodded. Alex circled and came back. "Hey, he's cute," she whispered. I looked at her and looked back at Alex. "He's really cute."

I frowned. "He's not *that* cute. His ears stick out," I muttered.

Alex made another U-turn and pedalled beside us. "Want another ride on Ginger, Keely? He needs exercise."

"Would I ever!"

"Saturday afternoon," Alex said. "See ya."

I stood grinning, watching Alex ride away.

Ginny stood with her hands on her hips in a manner reminiscent of her mother. "And the show?" she reminded me.

"No problem," I said. "You have Charlotte to go with." Ginny tried to stare menacingly through half-closed eyes but I just smiled and hummed, "Back in the saddle again, la, la."

Early Saturday afternoon I went into Patrick's room to investigate the state of his mind. Peggy had gone home for the weekend and he'd been having a bad morning. He had his eyes closed, pretending to be asleep. "Patrick," I whispered. He didn't answer. I tried again. "Are you asleep? Patrick?" I stood watching him. I leaned over and looked hard at his eyelids.

"Not. Any. More." He still had his eyes closed.

"I'm going riding."

Silence.

"Patrick?" I sat on the end of his bed.

"I'm still here."

"I could push you in your chair so you could come with me and watch."

"Don't be ridiculous." He opened his eyes.

"You could watch through the window, then."

"Could we just drop the whole subject?"

"Alex wants to be your friend. I know that's why he said I could ride his horse. So he could make up for leaving, that time. I mean, I *know*."

"I don't need Alex for a friend." He looked at me and looked away.

"He doesn't have to be your only friend. I'm sure there are lots of boys who. . . ."

"Why don't you put an ad in the paper. Wanted. Friend for a cripple. Must enjoy boredom."

"Patrick, why are you so . . . ever since we almost found Peggy's dead soldier, you've been so. . . . Patrick! That's an idea! Put an ad in the paper."

"If you do, I'll kill you."

"No, wait." I had jumped beyond Alex. I pictured a brief message, just a few words, in the classified section of, say, the Ottawa papers. Maybe the Toronto papers, too. "It could read: Derek, Peggy's love still alive in Channing, Ontario. Phone 737 for details."

Patrick snorted. "His name's not Derek, stupid. We made that up. Actually, Peggy told me what it was. It's Ian."

"Ian is even better than Derek. That's it, then. He's practically in the bag. When I come back we'll work out specific details. I won't be long." I dashed out in high gear.

Still running, I met Charlotte on Fairly Street. She was hurrying importantly towards Ginny's. She couldn't stop to talk, she said, because she had to meet her friend Ginny, and then they had to meet their friend Carol. And then they had to meet BUDDY DOLAN. Her voice deepened. "I think we all know why Buddy Dolan decided to come along."

I didn't. "Why?"

"Because I'm going, naturally. Word gets around, you know."

Several remarks ran through my head but I bit my tongue. I hurried on towards Alex and his horse. The riding lesson went well, I thought. Mounting and dismounting were old hat. Alex taught me to trot, an uncomfortably bumpy gait until you learn how to rise a bit in the saddle and miss half the bumps. Alex paid more attention to my feet in the stirrups and my hands on the reins than he did to me, the sister of Patrick, the boy he'd like once he got to know him.

"Patrick has a wheelchair now," I said as I bounced past on Ginger. Alex stood at the edge of the riding ring he had made, his hands behind his back, studying both Ginger and me.

"Keep your heels down, Keely," he replied.

"I got him outside as far as the front veranda."

"Toes in."

I rounded the ring again, jogging up to Alex. "You would have liked him before he got polio."

"Use your knees," Alex said.

I kept my heels down and my toes in and I used my knees like mad. I went round and round, popping up and down like the ducks in the duck-shoot game they have at the Rotary Fair. Finally Alex said we'd have to call it a day. He had work to do.

"The problem with Patrick is," I said, as Alex showed me how to remove Ginger's saddle and bridle, "he nearly died, and now he wishes he had."

"That's pretty stupid," Alex said. He rubbed the sweat off Ginger's chest and back with an old towel. "It's selfish. When somebody dies they take away something from everybody who loved them. Doesn't he ever think about you or your parents?"

I hesitated. "I don't know." I felt very young and small and nervous. I'd never had this kind of conversation with a boy before. Now was my chance to sound like an adult, say something serious, maybe gain some respect as a mature young woman. "He's disappearing," I said, and felt like a number-one idiot.

Alex threw the towel onto the fence. He nodded as though he knew what I meant. His eyes slanted down at the outside corners, the saddest eyes I'd ever seen.

"I'm sorry your father died," I blurted like a six-year-old. I ducked my head down and hid behind my bangs. I didn't have a hope of growing up.

"He had no choice," Alex said. He grabbed Ginger's halter and started to run with her up to the high pasture. He seemed angry.

I ran after him. "Wait! I need you to come back with me to talk to Patrick. You know the right things to say."

"What difference would it make?"

"He needs somebody like you."

"Then find somebody *like* me. *I* don't need him."

"I think he needs someone to push him around a little

bit. We can't. He just throws a fit."

"What do you think I am, a bully?"

"No, I think you're strong-willed, or something." Idiot remark of the year. "I mean, you don't play games with people." I puffed along beside Alex. He wouldn't slow down.

"I don't flatter people."

I stopped sharply. "Flatter! If you think I'm flattering you, buster, think again. I just meant . . . oh, never mind." I turned and tramped smartly towards home. I had pride too, after all.

"Wait!" Alex called. I kept going. "Hey, Keely!" With my chin jutting out I marched on. "Okay," Alex said, catching up. "I know what you mean. I'll come." He smiled apologetically.

I smiled back. I could handle a little moodiness.

We found Patrick in his wheelchair. Mother, looking worn to a frazzle, was putting his arms into the movable slings against violent protest from Patrick. He stopped yelling in surprise at the sight of Alex.

I said lamely, "Alex is here."

"It's nice of you to come again, Alex." Mother straightened slowly and pushed a hand into her back. She winced.

"Anything I can do to help?" Alex asked.

"No, not really, unless you and Keely want to push Patrick's chair outside."

"Forget it," said Patrick. "I'm not going outside."

"Well, into the back parlour, then."

"No."

"Well, where would you like to go?"

"To hell!"

Mother winced again, but said nothing.

Alex took the back of Patrick's chair and pushed it towards the door. Mother and I looked at each other, startled. "Get out of here," Patrick yelled when Alex paused to open the door. Alex ignored him and pushed the chair outside. Mother and I were right behind. "Get him out of here!" Patrick yelled. "Get him away from me!"

"Don't worry." Alex smiled back at my mother. "I'll be careful."

"But. . . ," Mother protested weakly.

"Help me get this rig down the steps, Keely." I hurried to do Alex's bidding. We bumped the heavy chair down the steps while Patrick shouted bloody murder. Mother fussed about whether he was warmly enough dressed. He had a blanket over his legs but only a sweater on top. "Looks fine to me," Alex said. He smiled reassurance at my mother. "We'll just go for a little walk and then we'll come back. Probably the fresh air will be good for him." Mother stood anxiously on the front veranda and watched Alex push the chair swiftly out to Fairly Street. I popped along, trying to keep up and trying to reassure Patrick that it would be all right. Patrick shrieked every rotten name he could think of at Alex. He ran out of breath finally and Alex slowed his pace. We were heading towards Sunny View Acres. Patrick got his wind again and took up where he had left off.

"Oh, shut up!" Alex said. "Don't be such a sissy!"

Patrick shut up instantly. I looked from Patrick to Alex and knew it had been some kind of magic.

"Wh-where are we going?" Patrick asked. If his voice wasn't precisely friendly, at least it was curious — and it wobbled as he was bustled along the uneven sidewalk.

"Sightseeing," Alex replied. He wheeled Patrick up the lane towards the Hodges' house. He rattled him up the ramp leading to the side porch, towards a man in a wheelchair talking to a man with crutches. Alex introduced both of us. Neither of the men seemed surprised by Patrick's chair. They said hello to Patrick and me and commented on the fine day.

"Got yourself a new job, Alex?" the man with crutches asked.

"Nope," said Alex. After a pause he said, "Got myself a

new friend."

The man in the wheelchair said to Patrick, "Gotta watch out for this lad, sonny. He likes to push people around. Har, har!" he laughed at his own joke. Patrick looked bewildered. The man went on, "Don't mind me, son, I like a few laughs now and again. When you got a friend like Alex, boy, you don't need enemies. That lad's tough. He said to me one day, he said, if you don't smarten up I'll take that wooden leg of yours and beat you over the head with it." Patrick's mouth fell open.

"That's what he said, and then he said, and if you don't stop whining I'll take your other wooden leg and ram it down your throat."

Patrick and I stared in awe at Alex.

Alex grinned. "Don't listen to him. Don't you know when your leg's being pulled?"

The man winked. "Hear about the man with the wooden leg? Wouldn' pull. Har, har, har!"

Patrick nearly smiled in spite of himself.

"That's it, sonny," the man said. "It's all right to laugh at yourself. At least one thing you and me's got that nobody else can claim, nobody laughs at us. People are good-hearted, mostly. They may feel sorry for us, but they don't laugh. On the other hand, we don't feel sorry for ourselves, so *we* can laugh our bloomin' heads off." He laughed his big, boisterous laugh again and I watched the corners of Patrick's mouth twitch upward. Alex laughed. I started to laugh and Patrick began to jiggle with silent laughter. He opened his mouth then and laughed out loud.

"Now, I'm not kidding you, me lad," the man said, wiping away tears of laughter. "You keep a sharp eye on the general here, and don't let him push you around." Alex already had the back of Patrick's chair and was turning it to push it back down the ramp. "Hey, didn't you hear me?" the man called, and this set Patrick off again.

The shadow of a smile lingered on Patrick's face all the way home. "What a character!" was all he said.

Alex left us at the front door. Before I pushed the wheelchair inside, Patrick called out, "Hey Alex! Drop in tomorrow sometime."

"Maybe," said Alex.

CHAPTER

11

On Sunday the sun slipped palely between my bedroom curtains, waking me. Looking out, I thought of sighs. The wind was rising. In spite of the weak sun, it was a grey day. Rain sat waiting.

Patrick awoke early and agreed to be put in his chair without the usual fuss. Mother stayed flat in bed to try to get rid of the kink in her back. Our father had to become nurse for the day.

I went to church with the Dicksons. Inching along the pew closer to me, Ginny whispered, "I've just finished writing a letter to Patrick. I'll probably write him another one in a couple of days. I'll either give them to you to deliver or else I'll drop them through your mail slot. Promise you won't let anyone but Patrick read them." A familiar stab of jealousy caused me to frown into my hymn-book. "Letters," Ginny breathed, "are so symbolic, don't you agree?"

I gave Ginny a bored look and turned to Hymn 389.

"Promise," Ginny whispered loudly, "or I'll tell Charlotte you love her clothes and wish you could borrow her pink dress."

Mrs. Dickson fixed us with a glare. Quickly we joined in the singing:

Almighty Father who dost give
The gift of life to all who live. . . .

I looked at Ginny and nodded agreement. She smiled and nodded back.

Of necessity, Father became not only nurse but family cook for the day. Our noon meal wasn't delicious, although Father kept telling us we were going to love it. He opened two tins of pork and beans (even one was too many). "Beans?" I said. Usually, on Sundays, we had roast chicken for our noon meal and a light supper later on.

"Beans," he replied, with a look that discouraged complaints. Then he opened a tin of sardines. Patrick and I sat across the table from each other, making faces when we thought Father wasn't looking. I curled my upper lip and Patrick let his tongue hang out. "There are starving children in Europe who would give their eye teeth for a meal like this," Father said.

"Sardines always put me in mind of giant bloodsuckers, don't you think?" I asked conversationally.

"No," Patrick said, "they aren't anything like bloodsuckers. They're more like dead minnows." Father put his fork down and said he had always liked sardines until now. "We need ketchup," Patrick said. I put a layer of ketchup over everything on both our plates, and to everyone's surprise he attempted to feed himself, with a fork specially designed with a loop handle.

After lunch we lounged around not doing much. We didn't mention Alex, but we were both waiting for him. I was, anyway. As the afternoon wore on I paced the floor, then went out to the veranda to look up and down Fairly Street. There was no sign of Alex. It had begun to rain; in fact, the sky seemed to open up and weep its heart out. The forsythia in front of the house took a beating. What had shone like a golden promise at Easter two weeks before stood stripped. The petals, a faded yellow now, lay scattered and muddy. I went back inside. Patrick, who had been sitting near the door, one ear cocked, looked hopefully at me. I shrugged. "Maybe he's busy."

Patrick said, "Maybe he forgot."

That evening Peggy phoned in sick. She thought she should stay home another day or two. She said her brother would drive her into Channing on Tuesday or Wednesday. This announcement met with long faces. Mother, who had got up for supper, was still moving about very gingerly. Father was worried about her back. He was slated to go to a week-long conference, and couldn't skip it as he was one of the speakers.

"I can cope," Mother assured him. "I'll go to the doctor, if necessary. There must be something he can give me for the pain."

Monday morning Patrick asked to stay in bed, partly to ease Mother's back, and partly because he was beginning to drift into a bad day; Alex's fault, I figured. I thought I could nip the bad day in the bud with my latest "search for Peggy's soldier" scheme. "About that classified ad," I said. No response. "Derek — I mean, Ian: Peggy's love still alive . . . you know." I was brushing my hair in front of Patrick's mirror.

"What about it?" No spark of interest but at least he had spoken.

"How should I go about it?" I was trying out two barrettes. Nothing.

"Come on, it was your idea, after all."

Finally Patrick said, "Go into the newspaper office on Duffel Street. They'll tell you. It'll cost you, you know."

"Cost me?" I hadn't considered the money factor. "How much?"

"No idea. Probably plenty."

I thought about my little box of savings, about my dream horse. And then I thought about Keely the Connor, charging through the mist fixing things, making everything better. "I have money," I said.

"Might as well save it," Patrick said. "It's a hare-brained idea from start to finish and it'll never work."

"It might."

"In a book. In a love story in a magazine. But not in real life, Keel. In real life you don't get happy endings." He closed his eyes.

"Wrong!" I yelled, startling him into opening his eyes. "Dead wrong! If that were true, nobody would do anything. Nobody would get up in the morning. Nobody would answer the phone or open the door or go anywhere. Nobody would take a dare." Patrick clamped his mouth shut and stared straight ahead. I'd said enough. But I went on anyway. "I think I'll put the ad in a whole bunch of papers, even if it uses up all my money. Maybe it'll work or maybe it won't, but I'll never know unless I do it."

I went back to putting the two barrettes in my hair. I stared at myself in Patrick's mirror. I looked like a ninny.

I came home for lunch to find Patrick staring vacantly at a spot on the wall. I called his name several times but couldn't get his attention. I flashed a white envelope before his face until finally he glanced at me with a deep sigh.

"A letter from Ginny. She asked me to deliver it."

Patrick raised and lowered his eyebrows in a who-cares expression.

"Want me to read it to you?"

"No."

"Want me to at least open it?"

"No."

"The flap's not very well stuck down."

"Oh, sure, you've probably already read it."

"No, honest. Ginny would kill me, or worse if I dared read it. Why don't you read it out loud while I hold it for you?"

"It's meant to be private. Give it here." He lightly tapped the index finger of his right hand on the cover.

"Private! *My* best friend and *my* only brother! Know what I hate about private? It always means 'Keely, keep out'. Isn't that just too symbolic!" I slapped the letter face down on Patrick's bed near his right hand and left without further argument.

Before going back to school I went up to check on Patrick. I stood quietly in the doorway. He was in a lather of sweat. I'd never seen him working so hard in all his life. He had managed to free the letter from the envelope and to inch it up the cover to perch on his stomach. I entered quietly. His head was raised slightly off the pillow, his eyes riveted to the piece of paper. He sank back exhausted. "I can only read the last five lines," he said when he could catch his breath.

I beamed at him. "That was better than any of your exercises. Want me to. . . ?"

"No. I'll find a way to read the whole thing by myself."

My errand at the newspaper office took longer than I expected. The woman behind the counter looked at me as if I were weird, but she didn't say it was a hare-brained idea. It was after four-thirty by the time I got home. I found Alex putting Patrick in his chair. Mother stood anxiously by, assisting where possible. Once Patrick was strapped in place, Alex said, "I have to put hay down for the horses. They're looking thin. Want to come?"

"Doesn't matter," Patrick said, but his eyes were suddenly brighter.

"Sorry I couldn't come yesterday. I never know from one day to the next how busy I'll be."

I watched Alex wheel Patrick towards the front door and open it. I had a sudden sense of something breaking with a snap as Patrick was bumped over the doorsill. The late-afternoon sun hit him at an angle, making him large as life. He wasn't a paper-thin ghost any more. I stood alone in the shadowy front hall watching them leave.

Alex stuck his head back in. "Hey Keely, aren't you coming?"

I wanted to say it didn't matter, but it did. I hurried after them.

At the side of the Hodges' house we were greeted by the man in the wheelchair, who asked us if we'd heard about the wooden cow. "Wouldn' milk, har, har." We laughed dutifully.

I took over the back of Patrick's chair now, and joggled him along to the stable to watch Alex fork down hay. "I want to show you something," I said. Patrick was pitched and rattled along the rutted lane to the driveshed, his head bouncing against the headrest. Alex followed us. When we got inside I swept my arms wide and said, "Look!" There was the breadwagon in all its faded glory. "A gypsy caravan," I announced. "If we painted over Quinlan's Bakery and took out the shelves, we could put a table and chairs in the back and we could hitch up old Bill and travel all over the place, telling people's fortunes and everything. We could take turns driving."

"Keely." Patrick had a practical tone to his voice.

"What?"

"Dumb idea."

"Wouldn't you like to drive that thing?"

"Sure. I'd like to fly to the moon, too."

"You could. I mean drive it. Couldn't he, Alex? I mean if we fixed it up with straps and everything." I jumped up on the wagon to show them what I meant. I pointed out a couple of areas where adjustments could be made.

"Wouldn't work. I couldn't hold the reins." Patrick didn't sound disappointed. But Alex began to warm to the project. "Slings," he said, "like on your wheelchair, with the reins attached somehow."

"Sounds dumb to me." Patrick changed the subject by asking Alex what he was studying in high school.

"But," I said.

"I'd like geometry, I think," Patrick said.

"But," I repeated.

Alex pushed Patrick out again into the glowing late afternoon, and wrestled his heavy chair back along the lane. They were making plans. Alex would bring some of his books around to Patrick.

Hartley Hodge stood sullenly at the end of his lane and watched our approach. He moved away from me and closer to Alex, staring curiously at Patrick.

"Hey kid," he said to Patrick. "What happened to you?"

"An old war injury," Patrick replied. Hartley stared dully at him so Patrick went on. "See, I was flying this Lancaster bomber when we were hit, see, and I baled out but my parachute didn't open, so I fell about a million feet, and then. . . ."

"He's lying," said the astute Hartley. There were no flies on him.

"Come around and see my medals sometime," Patrick laughed.

I felt almost grateful to Hartley Hodge, juvenile delinquent though he would always be in my books. He had made Patrick laugh.

After Alex had left us at the door, Patrick said, "Funny how Alex turned out to be a pretty good egg. He was just moody, I guess."

"He's not moody, he's nice."

Patrick looked at me with narrowed eyes and said, "Mm," whatever that was supposed to mean.

Monday, Peggy phoned again. She had the measles, she told Mother. "How's Patrick?" She was nearly in tears with concern. Mother assured her that Patrick seemed to have been spared. Patrick was near the phone. "Let me talk," he said. "Look." He had his arms in their slings more or less cradled in front of his chest. "Put the phone here." Mother propped the heavy black receiver in his arms and Patrick tilted his head as far as he could. "Peggy," he shouted, "I'm holding the phone by myself. Speak up, I can't hear you." Then he could hear her and his eyes lit up. "Peggy," he yelled, "I'm sorry you got the measles, but listen. I'm holding the phone all by myself and talking to you." We could all hear Peggy yell congratulations at her end. "Hey, listen," he said, "I bet this is just about as good as Alexander Graham Bell's first telephone call."

Father left early Monday for his conference. Caring for Patrick was taking its toll on our mother's back, so she left me in charge after school while she went to the doctor. Alex came over and together in the back parlour we taped an old kneesock around the charcoal pencil Ginny had given Patrick, which had lain untouched on his dresser ever since. The pencil fit loosely into Patrick's hand and with the aid of his slings he was able to attempt drawing triangles. He bit his tongue in his effort to keep the lines straight.

When Mother came in she looked pale and worried, and dropped her bombshell. "The doctor says I'm not to do any more lifting. We have to hire a nurse until Peggy comes back." Light from the parlour window seemed to etch lines into her face.

Patrick looked up sharply. I looked warily at her. "Who?" I asked.

"I'm afraid Mrs. Whinney is the only person available."

The pencil fell out of Patrick's frail grip. Alex glanced at each of us, puzzled. I said to him, "You're going to start believing in witches when you meet Mrs. Whinney."

"Now, now," Mother said, "I think we owe her a second chance. We were all a little nervous about the prospect of having a stranger live here and look after Patrick. She can't be all that bad or the doctor wouldn't have suggested her. We may as well grin and bear it, it's only for a week or so."

Mrs. Whinney moved in late that evening, in time to put Patrick to bed. Nobody grinned, but we did our best to bear it. Mother had to spend a large part of each day in bed, and Mrs. Whinney didn't seem to find it amusing to have two invalids on her hands. Patrick grew more and more sullen as each day passed, and spent more and more time in bed staring at the wall. I came home from school on Friday to find him in bed in his pyjamas and Mrs. Whinney carrying away his dinner tray.

"How come?" I asked Patrick when Mrs. Whinney had vacated the room. I moved Mrs. W's stack of *Silver Screen* magazines from *my* chair, plunked them on the floor and sat studying him.

He opened his eyes and gazed listlessly at the wall. "It's easier, I guess."

"Easier!" I jumped up. The magazines somehow got kicked under Patrick's dresser.

"Easier for her Royal Weirdship, I mean. I don't think she can stomach the sight of me trying to feed myself, so this is her way out. She'll feed me up here, then eat like the lady she is in the dining-room."

"I'm going to tell Mother." I turned, about to march out.

"Don't. Mother's feeling bad enough. What's the use, anyway? If I complain, Whinney just finds some way of punishing me. Yesterday, before you got home, she wouldn't let Alex in to see me because I swore at her."

"Patrick! Why did you swear at her?" I came closer.

"Which of the hundred and one reasons do you want? She won't leave a night-light on because I'm too old. She won't let me listen to the radio after ten because I'm too young. She wouldn't . . . look, do you want me to keep on? She makes me feel powerless. My comfort depends on her mood. She wouldn't set up my bookholder just now because I'm a liar."

"You! A liar? I thought I was the only one to hold that

title." I grinned, hoping he'd remember the skunks.

He almost smiled. "I told her this morning the doctor was going to pay a visit to check up on her. It worked for most of the day. She was almost nice to me. But then she got suspicious and asked Mother. So here I am, paying for my sins."

"Well, it won't be much longer. At least we know there's a time limit." I tried to smooth the pillow under his head.

"No there isn't. Not really. You know, for a few days last week I thought life might almost be worth living, but it isn't. I know that now. There will always be a Mrs. Whinney out there waiting for me. I *am* powerless. Anybody can do anything they like with me and I can't stop them. What's the use in even trying to do a few little things? It's not worth it when you realize you'll always be a dependent baby. Why did Peggy have to get the measles? Why couldn't it have been me? I might have died."

"Patrick, don't talk like that." I stood looking into his sad face.

"Go away."

"Did you hear about the wooden horse?"

"Go away."

"Wouldn' go."

"I just want to die and get it over with." He closed his eyes. They had grey circles under them, and I could tell by the way he was flaring his nostrils that he was trying to keep from crying. He lay there, making me think once again of a puppet with broken strings, making *me* feel powerless. If I could only patch him up, tie knots in the strings. . . .

Downstairs, Mrs. Whinney was washing Patrick's few dishes. "He's sickening for something, that lad," she said when I came into the kitchen. "Didn't touch a morsel of his supper."

"Why don't you put him in his chair and let him feed himself?" I tried to make it a question, not an accusation. I was learning that Mrs. Whinney had to be "handled".

Mrs. Whinney shook her head. "Won't co-operate. Stubborn, spoiled little liar, that lad. I can't abide a liar. And if he don't want to do something, why, he just throws a temper tantrum." She removed the pink box of pills from her apron pocket and shook it in my face. "Took two of these pills to calm him down yesterday morning. I'd have given him two more in the afternoon, but you never know what'd make him sick or kill him." She put the pills back in her pocket. I scowled at the floor.

On Saturday, after lunch, Mother went to see the doctor again. I took the opportunity to climb the back fence into Sunny View Acres. I wanted to ask Alex to help me put Patrick into his chair. "Okay," Alex agreed, "but I can't stay long. I have to get back to work." We walked quietly past the living-room, where Mrs. Whinney was glued to the radio listening to "Grand Central Station".

Patrick took no notice of our arrival in his room. He looked at Alex, finally, but his eyes didn't light up.

"We're going to get you up in your chair," I said.

"Why?"

"Don't you want to sit up?"

"No."

Alex looked concerned. "Would you rather stay in bed?"

"No."

Alex and I looked helplessly at each other. "What do you want to do, Patrick?" I asked.

"Die."

"I can't stay long now," Alex tried to make his voice jovial, "but we'll get you up and I'll come back later when I finish my work. Okay?"

"Why bother?"

Alex lifted Patrick under the arms and I took his legs. Together we carried him downstairs to his chair in the back parlour. As we passed the living-room I gave Mrs. Whinney a quick explanation, but she waved us away with a shush and put her ear closer to the radio. Alex strapped Patrick into his chair and I put his arms into the slings. Patrick's head lay against the headrest. He closed his eyes.

"Hey!" said Alex. He gave Patrick a playful tap. "Get your medals out. I may bring old Hartley Hodge over with me." Patrick opened his eyes and looked in Alex's direction. His eyes looked dead. Alex reflected for a moment. "I've got a better idea. Put on a sweater, Patrick, and Keely can push you over yonder. You can watch her ride Ginger."

I looked eagerly at Patrick, hope in my eyes.

Patrick's face was a study in despair.

Alex had to leave. "I'll go over the back fence again," he said sadly. I saw him to the kitchen door.

In the kitchen I poured ginger ale for Patrick. I put the glass on his tray in front of him with an extra-long straw. If he felt like it he could tilt his head and drink through the straw by himself. He chose not to. I tried to find something more exciting than dandelions dotting the back lawn to point out to him, but couldn't.

We heard Mrs. Whinney's heavy steps coming along the hall towards us. Her program must have ended. She entered the back parlour waving an opened envelope in one hand and a piece of paper in the other. "Well, well," she said, "our young Master Patrick seems to be getting love letters delivered through the front door."

Patrick's face became livid; I felt all the colour drain from mine.

Mrs. Whinney took no notice. "*My* dear Patrick, the young lady writes. Isn't that sweet, and she signs it, with *all* my symbolic love. Well, now. So, Patrick has a girlfriend," she trilled.

"Bitch!" breathed Patrick, his face on fire. "You bitch!" he shrieked. With the little bit of movement he could muster he began to sway. He got his arms swaying together and together they banged his ginger ale glass with enough force to knock it crashing to the floor. He screamed at Mrs. Whinney louder than he'd ever screamed before. He cursed her and damned her and sent her to hell and back many times over. He shrieked until he coughed and then shrieked some more.

"You little monster!" Mrs. Whinney yelled at him. She took the pink cardboard box of pills out of her apron pocket and slammed it down on his tray. Half of them spilled out through the end flap, which had sprung open on impact. "Wouldn't I just like to wallop your backside!" She got down on her thick knees to start picking up the broken glass. Out of breath, Patrick stopped screaming.

"Don't just stand there with your eyes hanging out," she said to me. "Go and get him a glass of water, and bring a rag to mop up this mess." She was down on all fours now, scrabbling under Patrick's chair and reaching under the furniture to pick up the shattered glass. Patrick was silent. From the kitchen I could hear her harangue.

"You've gone just about one step too far this time, my lad. Any youngster your age who can't take a bit of teasing ought to get the back of somebody's hand. The very idea!" She got no reaction from Patrick.

I was back with the water and a rag.

"Give him two of them pills now, Keely, while I get this cleaned up." She dumped a handful of broken glass into the wastebasket.

"But he's calmed down now," I argued.

"Can nobody do what they're told around here?" Mrs. Whinney sounded at her wit's end.

Patrick began to swear again, his voice shrill. His face turned red and he began to choke. I looked at the spilled pills on his tray. I thought there had been more. His shrieks pierced my mind. "Give him his pills!" Mrs. Whinney ordered. "Or do you want him to burst a blood vessel right before your eyes?" She left the room with the soaked rag.

I put two pills in Patrick's mouth and tilted the water glass for him to drink. There was immediate silence. "Thank you," Patrick whispered hoarsely. With his index finger he dabbed water from the corner of his lip. He put his head back against the headrest, exhausted.

I put the glass down and stared again at the few remaining pills on his tray. "You didn't swallow any of these, did you, Patrick?"

"What?" Patrick still had his eyes closed.

"The pills on your tray."

"No."

"Are you telling the truth?"

"Don't be ridiculous!" he shouted.

From the kitchen Mrs. Whinney called, "Keely, you leave that lad alone now or he'll never calm down. Run along and ride your precious horse, or whatever it is you do next door."

Patrick attempted a smile. "You heard Her Ladyship. Go ride your precious horse." I stood looking anxiously at Patrick. I put the spilled pills back in the box.

"It's all right," Patrick said. "Mother will be home any minute. Go on." He closed his eyes and breathed deeply and evenly. He looked as though he would sleep now. Reluctantly I moved towards the door. He called to me and I turned around. He seemed to look intently at me, as if he were memorizing me. "See you later," he said.

I was not in high spirits at Sunny View Acres. Charlotte and I played with the kittens for a while. Charlotte announced that she had given her orange kitten an additional name. I thought three names unnecessarily cumbersome and said so, but I asked what it was. "Patrick Marmalade Puss. Puss for short."

"Oh, brother," I sighed.

I went in search of Alex but he was still tied up with his chores. He was helping one of the veterans restore the hen-house. I watched for a while but couldn't get interested.

"How about a game of Snakes & Ladders?" Charlotte asked. I ignored her. Charlotte's awful brother rode past on his bike, giving me a wide berth and speeding down the lane towards Fairly Street. I went into the driveshed and sat in the breadwagon. Charlotte told me I was no fun. I tried to imagine how you would harness a horse to the wagon but couldn't, so I got down and went back out. I had just about decided to go and tell Alex I was going back home when Hartley came back up the lane, pedalling hard. His little cupid's bow mouth looked almost wide with shock. He rode up to me and stopped with his bike between us.

"What's your problem?" I asked crossly.

He opened and closed his lips a couple of times before any words came out. "I guess your brother musta died, eh?"

"What are you talking about?" My tone was menacing. Hartley dragged his bike farther away. "What do you mean?" I shouted at him.

"The hearse was at your house, eh, and they carried your brother out and your mother was crying right out loud. I saw the whole thing."

I blazed at him, "You're lying!"

"I am not."

I felt as if my face would shatter. Stumbling at first, I began to run.

CHAPTER

12

I tore open our front door and ran wildly through the house, calling Patrick, calling my mother. The house's answering silence pounded inside my head. Patrick's chair was empty. Upstairs, his bed was empty. Mrs. Whinney's suitcase, which had stood open on a trestle in Peggy's room, was gone.

I found myself back outside. My arms and legs moved with a will of their own. My brain was splintering into fragments. I felt as though needles were being driven into me, all over my body, but especially into my head. Patrick had disappeared and I hadn't. Nothing should exist without Patrick. Now I felt that I was receding, shrinking; my world, fading, vaporizing, was disappearing too. I could hear a scream going on inside me, but no sound came from my mouth.

A boy was hurrying up the street towards me, dressed in faded overalls that were too short. I could see him, but I couldn't focus on him until he was close. "Keely!" Alex called. "Hey, Keely!" I saw his tall, strong body shimmer gracefully towards me, one foot in front of the other, his arms swinging loosely at his sides, his hands useful and powerful. The space around his perfect body glowed.

I lowered my head and charged him like a billy-goat, nearly knocking him off his feet. I flailed at him with both fists. I kicked him. I began to scratch at his face with my nails until he hit me back. Again I lunged at him, tears streaming down my face and an animal howl coming from deep inside. Alex was quicker this time. He grabbed my arms and pinned them close. Still I struggled, lashing out with my feet. As though he didn't know what else to do, he pulled me to him and held me in a rib-crushing bearhug. I felt the impossibility of doing further damage. Gradually I gave up the struggle and my howls turned to sobs. I had to gulp for air, so tightly did Alex have me gripped to him.

He loosened his hold, finally, and said soothing things, the way he would to an injured puppy. He even patted my head once or twice. He began to move away, but I stayed close to him and dried my cheeks on the bib of his overalls. At last I pushed him away, my breath still coming in little shuddering hiccups.

"Keely," Alex said, "what happened?"

"Pat-Patrick," I began.

"What about him?"

"He's gone. He's dead."

"That's what Hartley said. I didn't believe him." Neither of us could say anything else. We couldn't look at each other. Alex glanced back at the house, the front door gaping open. "We better try to locate your mother," he said.

The next few minutes crept like hours. The next few hours took days. My mother talked to me from a hospital phone. Patrick, it turned out, had been picked up not in a hearse but in an ambulance. He wasn't dead, but in his already weakened condition he was dangerously ill. He was still unconscious.

"But what happened?" I needed to know details.

Mother hesitated. "Mrs. Whinney gave him two more pills," she blurted finally.

"But why? I. . . ."

"After you left, she asked him if you had given him his pills. He apparently said no, so Mrs. Whinney got out two

more pills for him. Then he must have thought better of his
lie because he admitted that you *had* given him his pills.
Well, Mrs. Whinney didn't believe him. She said he was
always lying to her. She jammed two more pills down his
helpless throat."

"I could murder her," I roared.

Mother continued, "I had just come in. He called me. He
sounded . . . panicky." Her voice faltered. "He . . . said the
pills had spilled. He was getting drowsy. He thought he had
managed to swallow two or three . . . he wasn't sure."

I waited for her to go on. She began, "The doctor doesn't
know if. . . ." She was crying now. I was crying. I wanted to
go to the hospital but she told me to stay at home. Father
was on his way back from the conference. The Dicksons
would stay with me. Peggy had been notified.

I sat numbly in the living-room with the Dicksons. Mr.
Dickson stayed for a while, but left, finally, when Alex left.
Mrs. Dickson made tea but nobody drank it. The phone rang
and we all jumped. It was only Mrs. Hodge. Word had got
round. She asked Mrs. Dickson if I would like Charlotte to
keep me company. Maybe a game of Chinese checkers
would help to pass the time. Mrs. Dickson relayed the
message. "If Charlotte comes over here," I replied, "I'll take
an axe to her head."

"Thank you, no," Mrs. Dickson said into the phone. She
talked for a little longer, answering Mrs. Hodge's questions.

"If I'd said that," Ginny whispered, "she would have murdered me."

I shrugged.

Early in the evening the phone rang once more. Everyone
started again, but fear of the worst caused each of us to hesitate to answer it. I picked it up. "What is it?" I asked
abruptly. During the next moment I felt light-headed. I
couldn't make myself say anything. I managed to gulp,
"Thank you," and hung up.

Mrs. Dickson and Ginny stood tensely beside me. "They think he's going to be okay," I whispered. I ran upstairs to the bathroom to be sick.

I visited Patrick in hospital. His dark hair stood out against his own pallor and the snowy sheets. I tried to say something but my voice wouldn't work. I just stood and looked into his eyes. He looked back at me, not smiling, not angry, not even willing me to disappear by closing his eyes. I bent over him, brushed the hair from his forehead and kissed him lightly. I moved back quickly, expecting him to yell, "Get her away from me." He didn't. He just kept looking at me. A tear slipped across his cheek and dampened his pillow. I couldn't handle this. I closed my eyes and willed *my* emotions to disappear.

I spent most nights lying awake trying to sort things out, tidy up my thoughts. On the one hand, I rejoiced that he was alive. On the other, I knew how he must feel. Like a failure. He didn't know how to live and he didn't know how to die. I sat with Ginny late one afternoon on her front steps, hunched over my knees, trying to look the thing squarely in the face. "I tried to make him want to live and I failed," I said.

"It was Mrs. Whinney's fault," Ginny said. "And anyway, he's okay."

"He's okay, but. . . ."

"Keely, you can't be his guardian angel for ever."

That night I got on the phone and asked the operator for long distance. When Peggy came on I said, "I tried to make him *want* to live. What did I do wrong?"

"You didn't do anything wrong," she said. "Patrick flirted — cautiously maybe, but flirted nevertheless — with the means of escaping his life. Whether it was his fault or Mrs. Whinney's doesn't matter, because he was falling in love with the idea of dying. You're not magic, Keely. Remember that old impossibility factor you mystified us with once? Maybe you *can't* control his destiny. If there is such a thing."

I tried to picture Peggy recovering from the measles in her own house up the Valley, with her father and her brother, but I couldn't. I'd never been there. She sounded so different on the phone, a bit the way she had the day she read Patrick's teacup and stopped, saying it had given her a headache. Strained, I guess, was how she sounded. Patrick had said, "There's something bad in there," but Peggy had said she didn't believe in bad fortunes. I wondered if she did now. I didn't ask her. It was too hard a question. We said goodbye and both hung up.

On Saturday I climbed the fence into Sunny View Acres and wandered up to the horses on the brow of the high pasture. I felt as though I'd come to say goodbye to them, although none of us was going anywhere. All three came over to me looking for treats. Lola clumped off in a huff when I held out an empty hand, but Ginger stayed to have his forehead rubbed and old Bill leaned his big chin on my shoulder. I left them there without looking back at them and started to climb over the fence. Then I heard Alex calling me so I waited, straddling the fence. When he got close enough he said, "When is Patrick coming home?"

"In a few days."

"That's good."

"Mm-hmm."

"Keely?"

"What?"

"You don't sound very happy."

I was sitting on the top rail. I looked down at Alex, who was leaning into the fence, studying the expression on my face as if he had to write an exam on it. I was going to say, "I'm happy," but instead I said, "I dared Patrick to get a grip on life but he backed away from it. I tried to wrap him up in my life but he shook loose and nearly escaped."

Alex didn't say anything. I was glad he didn't because, what could he say? What he did was take hold of my foot that was hanging down beside him and give it a shake. This made me smile. I said I had to go and he said he had to go too.

I knew something now, something I didn't feel like discussing with anyone. The silver stallion was a fairy-tale. It had no place in real life.

Saturday night Ginny asked me over but I said I couldn't go, I had a toothache. I didn't really. I had an ache of some sort but I couldn't pin it down to an exact spot. I should have told Ginny I felt like a tooth with an ache in the middle of it. I was in my room mulling all this over when my mother came in.

"Why are you sitting here staring at the wall?"

"Was I?" She wanted me to go down and listen to "Share the Wealth" with her. "Maybe later," I said. I went to bed instead.

Sunday afternoon Alex came over and asked if I wanted to ride Ginger. I was in the back parlour in front of the window, although not actually looking out. "Nah," I replied.

He leaned against the windowsill. "How come?"

"I can't see the point of it. Just popping along on some four-legged animal. Where does it lead?"

"I could teach you to canter."

"What's that?"

"Next thing to a flat-out gallop."

I looked at him, almost tempted, but turned back to the window. "Nah," I said, "it's a bore." I closed my eyes.

Alex left then, as though his feelings were hurt. I nearly went after him but didn't. What was the point?

Mother came in and said she had just been talking to Peggy. "She'll get here tomorrow, about the same time as Patrick." She was smiling, so I smiled too. She pointed out the window. "Look."

Lola frisked about in the distance, then lay down with all four legs in the air, rolling in the new spring grass. Ginger ignored her, but old Bill seemed curious. He ambled over and put his head down close to hers. Lola snorted and rolled onto her side, tucking her legs under her. She was back up again and trotting. Bill trotted after her while Ginger munched grass. Mother looked at me so I smiled.

Mother's back was giving her less trouble now. "We'll have something special for dinner on Monday," she said. "What do you think Patrick would like?"

"I dunno."

"It's nice that he's getting home well ahead of your birthday."

"Guess so."

"He can help you plan it."

"Plan it?"

"Well, a thirteenth birthday is pretty special, isn't it?"

"I dunno."

"Keely, what's wrong?"

"I dunno."

I came home from school Monday to find Patrick tucked into his own bed and Peggy ensconced in her rocker, knitting. It was as though nothing had happened, no time had elapsed. The world had not almost stopped. I stood in the doorway and talked for a minute, then moved along to my own room. "I have a lot of homework," I said.

It was much the same on Tuesday. Peggy asked why Old Man Leach was piling the homework on all of a sudden. "I dunno," I said.

The next day Patrick was in his chair when I came home. "Come here," he called from the back parlour. "They're going to make this into my room," he said when I went in. He looked longer; his knees jutted out farther beneath the tray of his chair.

"That's nice."

"If you rode Ginger in the field, I could watch."

"I don't ride much any more."

"Why not?"

"What's the point?" I watched a fly buzzing to life, trapped between the inside window and the storm window. Father hadn't put all the screens on yet.

Patrick said, "You know what the point is."

"Oh, big deal. Heroes ride horses. Sure. That was in the olden days when we were little kids." I turned to face Patrick. "Who thinks about that stuff any more?" Maybe I had grown, too. I seemed to be looking at Patrick from a great height.

"I do," he said quietly.

"I bet." I turned again to the window, peering through it at an angle. Something new and white near the fence looked like the first trilliums just coming out. I'd been looking for them almost since the snow melted.

"I can't stand you being angry with me, Keely."

I denied being angry. I opened the window and flipped up the slat covering the three air holes in the storm window, allowing the fly an escape route.

Patrick cleared his throat. "First of all, I'm sorry."

"What for?"

"I guess I'm sorry about those spilled pills. I shouldn't have. . . . I didn't know Whinney wouldn't believe me. I didn't know she'd give me more."

"I didn't know the gun was loaded." My voice was sarcastic as all get out. I slammed the inside window shut.

"What?"

"Nothing."

"You *are* angry."

"Of course I am. Who do you think you are, God Almighty, deciding who'll live and who'll die?"

"It's my life."

"Maybe, but it's pretty well mixed up with mine." It was

Patrick's turn to be silent. "I thought I was dying too, and I didn't want to," I said.

"I didn't die."

"Obviously." I'd heard enough. I closed my eyes.

"Keely, listen. You know how they say your whole life flashes before your eyes when you think you're going to die? Well, it doesn't. At least mine didn't. When I got those pills into my mouth I thought that I was finally in charge of things and that with the two more Whinney told you to give me I might just make my escape."

I opened my eyes and stood there grinding my teeth.

"Hey, there was nothing you or anyone else could do," he added.

"I could have stayed around. I could have kept an eye on you. I could have booted Whinney from here to kingdom come."

"No, you couldn't have. Anyway. I thought, big deal. Who cares? Until I saw you walking out the door."

I turned and looked at him. I felt that toothache thing in my eyes now.

"When the old witch crammed those pills down my throat, I saw you again. I kept seeing you walk out that door. I knew two things then. One, I was maybe going to die, and two, I didn't want to." He stopped and swallowed. He looked away.

"You didn't want to?"

"Bad as my life seems, it's a life. It's got light and air and colours in it. It's got people in it I care about. Then I started getting groggy and I started swearing under my breath. I thought, now I'll never find out what happens."

"What do you mean, what happens?"

"You know. How things turn out. You'd keep on going, you and Ginny and Alex and old Charlotte and everybody. And I'd stop. Like a broken movie film. Only they wouldn't turn on the lights and splice the film and start her up again.

I'd be left . . . in the dark. I'd never find out what happened next. I'd never know if there was a happy ending. I couldn't stand the thought of a cold, dark emptiness. I was getting really woozy by this time. I thought Mother was home but I wasn't sure. I just started hollering for her anyway, and that's all I remember before I blanked out." I stood contemplating him, nodding my head, not saying anything. "Are you still mad at me?" he asked.

"Yes." I had to admit it. "This has been the worst part of my life so far."

"Mine too."

"Good." I stood, hands on hips Mrs. Dickson style, and glared at him.

"But I'm sorry."

I looked down. The words sounded so lame compared to what he was sorry for. I shrugged. What other words are there? "Yeah, well. . . ."

"You can't stay cross for ever."

"Maybe not."

"It's all right to smile once in a while, you know. You can even yell at me, if you want." I wasn't in the mood for either smiling or yelling. Patrick managed to get his old teasing voice back. "Guess it would have spoiled your birthday party, eh?"

I glanced at him, realizing he was trying to get me going. I almost smiled. "Maybe," I said, "and maybe not."

"Old Keel, trying to decide whether to blow out the candles or blow her nose."

"Oh, shut up." I grinned at him. He grinned back. Siamese twins, joined at the mind. We were almost back on the old stompin' ground.

Within hours the insults were flying freely. Eventually what passed for normal life in our family returned. We all felt Patrick's near catastrophe was better put behind us. We had shed all our tears.

CHAPTER

13

Patrick and I made treks out to check the progress of the trilliums growing in profusion in the woodsy corner of our backyard near the fence. We went out nearly every day for a week. There were pale pink hepaticas among the dappled roots of trees, and in the sunny grass, violets. The garden had that brand-new smell of freshly turned earth and the rhubarb was almost high enough to pick. I pulled out a slender stalk, wiped off the sand and crunched into it.

Patrick winced. "How can you do that?"

I had to admit it was tart enough to make my teeth curl. But I wanted to eat it. Spring was here; it wasn't enough just to see it and smell it.

My birthday was a little over a week away. I was sitting one evening with Patrick and Mother in the living-room, half listening to "Wayne and Shuster" on the radio and half planning a party. Father was at a meeting and Peggy was at the movies with Laurence Saunders.

"I meant to say no when he asked me," she had said, "but somehow it came out sounding like yes."

Mother had said, well, well, with a knowing tone. Patrick and I gave each other significant looks. I muttered to Patrick, "That soldier better show up soon, before it's too late." I had enough money to run the ad in the Toronto papers just one more week and that was all. If nothing came of it, well, I wouldn't exactly stop believing in happy endings, but I wouldn't lay any huge bets on them. Or trade them for a horse. What if Peggy married Laurence Saunders? That *could* be a happy ending. But it sure wouldn't be romantic.

It was chilly for a mid-May evening and was beginning to drizzle. We sat in the cheer of a coal fire, probably our last until next fall. It crackled in the small fireplace. "Who do you want to invite to your party?" Mother asked me.

"I'm inviting mature and sophisticated friends only."

"Name one," Patrick said.

"Carol Katski for one, I guess. And also Linda Ford. She's not really a friend, but she's sophisticated. And of course Ginny."

"Sophistication takes on a whole new meaning," Patrick said.

"Did I ask your opinion?"

"Now, now," Mother frowned at Patrick. To me she said, "You can't very well leave out Charlotte." I screwed up my mouth but agreed to invite Charlotte. Mother studied me carefully, sizing me up, length and width. "I think your red and green Margaret Rose plaid dress would do you very nicely one more year."

"That freak of a thing," I wailed. "It's way too short. It makes me look like I'm walking on stilts. Ultra-thin stilts."

"It did last year too," Patrick offered, "but you didn't care." He seemed to sit straighter now, his head not even touching the headrest. Twice a day Peggy made him do strengthening exercises. He didn't put up a fight about it anymore. In fact once or twice I found him exercising on his own, working on getting his hand up to his head. More than anything he wanted to be able to comb his own hair. He hates the way Peggy does it. I offered to comb it but he just yelled at me to mind my own business. Peggy said once she could feel flickers of movement in some of his leg muscles, but Patrick told her not to talk about it. He was afraid to hope.

"I didn't care about the dress last year because I was only a child." I tossed my head at Patrick the way Katherine Hepburn does when she's being haughty. I like Katherine Hepburn even though she doesn't have a horse.

The radio program ended and Mother said she had to finish her ironing. She stood up but hesitated. "Keely," she said, "did you want to invite boys?"

"Boys!" I think I made the word sound almost foreign to the language. I concentrated on nibbling off a hangnail.

"Well, I just wondered. . . ."

"I don't know any boys."

"What about Buddy Dolan?" Patrick teased.

"I'd sooner invite Jack the Ripper."

"You know Alex," Mother said.

"Oh, him. He's too old."

"He's the same age I am," Patrick said.

"I mean, he seems older. If he saw me wearing that dumb dress and trying to pretend I was sophisticated and everything, he'd just laugh. I'd be embarrassed."

"Did he make you feel embarrassed when you used to ride his horse?" Patrick asked.

"No, but now . . . I just don't want him to see me looking goofy." I took the poker and stirred up the fire, which made my face hot.

From the doorway, Mother said, "If you feel you need a new dress, we can manage it."

"It's not just the dress. It's my stupid-looking looks. If I could just get my hair to go into the upsweep." I demonstrated, pulling my hair up and away from my face. Most of it fell back down.

"There's nothing wrong with your looks, Keely," my mother said. "You have lovely high cheekbones and beautiful eyes."

"Oh, sure," I crossed my eyes, sucked in my cheeks and

made fish-lips at Mother. She shook her head and went to do her ironing.

I slouched into the chair, sighing, then got up with another sigh and looked out into the darkness. The drizzle had worked itself into a steady downpour. I raked up the fire and added another small piece of cannel-coal. It snapped with a spray of sparks. "Watch what you're doing," Patrick said.

I had other things on my mind. "I wish people had little taps built in, so that when they found themselves thinking too hard about something they could turn off a tap and just stop thinking. Or if they found themselves getting exhausted by feeling embarrassed or sad or lonely, they could turn the tap off, or partway off, and just have emotions in small drips. Or if. . . ."

"I wish people came equipped with little knobs, so that when they ran off at the mouth you could turn them off like a radio."

"Creep!" I watched the fire in silence.

Patrick watched the fire in silence too, but he looked as though he was making up his mind about something. "Maybe I will go to the show, after all." He was talking aloud to himself.

"Huh?"

"Saturday afternoon. Go get the paper and see what's on."

"Huh?"

"It's on the radiator in the hall."

"How come you want to go see movies all of a sudden?"

"Something to do."

"But. . . ."

"It's probably not so bad being stared at. It might be kind of interesting watching people pretend they're not really staring. I'd have to sit at the back because of my wheelchair so I wouldn't be all that obvious."

"If Ginny helped me, I guess I could get your chair up and down all the curbs and steps."

"You don't have to take me. I'm going with Alex."

"Since when?"

"Since yesterday afternoon. He said he was going Saturday with some other guy and I could come along if I wanted. He has the day off. I said I might if there was anything good on. Get the paper."

I returned with the paper and felt like just any old younger sister. "Can't I go?"

"Go if you like. You'll be the only girl."

I frowned and turned to the back page. "Roy Rogers is on," I read, "king of the cowboys, and Trigger, smartest horse in the movies. And Gabby Hayes is in it, and The Sons of the Pioneers, and way down here at the bottom it says, 'with Dale Evans'. You wouldn't like it. Now here's the coming attraction. 'Blue Skies' with Bing Crosby and Fred Astaire. That sounds more your style."

"It's been a long time since I saw Roy Rogers."

"It'll be dumb."

"So, nobody's forcing you to go."

"Fine, then, I won't." I left Patrick to the fire, the lamplight and the newspaper. "I have homework," I said.

Mr. Leach had told us to memorize the whole of "La Belle Dame sans Merci" but I hadn't planned on doing it. I'd found that when he was looking around to nail someone to recite memory work, the best thing to do was sit there looking confident, smug even. He always picked someone else. But I decided, what the heck, and opened the book. I read the first verse and thought, yes.

> O what can ail thee, knight at arms,
> Alone and palely loitering?
> The sedge has wither'd from the lake,
> And no birds sing.

"Alone and palely loitering" said it all. I memorized the thing while I got ready for bed, and didn't think once about Patrick and Alex going to the show together and not including me.

Alex didn't even enter my mind as I snapped "La Belle Dame" shut and climbed into bed. I never really liked Alex that much, anyway. I switched out the light. His ears stuck out. Just a little. When he smiled. I punched my pillow into shape. The last person in the world I was going to lose any sleep over was Alex Dalby. I lay there staring into the dark.

Saturday, Peggy hummed a happy tune while she got Patrick ready to go out. "You're growing, young man," she said. "The next time your mother goes shopping, new trousers are in order." I could hear the banter from my room. I heard Peggy tease him about growing a beard. "If you don't speed along with your exercises you won't be able to shave when the need arises. And if I tried it, I'd probably cut your throat."

"Peggy!" Patrick sounded as though life had become a serious undertaking. He was, after all, confronting the public.

The boys arrived for him sounding shy and uncommunicative. I kept well out of everyone's way, listening. Yes, they could manage. No, they didn't need help. Yes. No. Yes. Goodbye. Alex pushed Patrick's chair speedily. John, Alex's friend, made a joke about a driver's licence and they all relaxed. Alone and palely loitering, I watched them from the bay window in the living-room. Three boys going to the show. How normal! They didn't need me. Why would they? They hadn't mentioned my name, not even to say, sure glad old Keely's not coming. I was forgotten. Somebody's sister. Somebody's former friend.

I could have gone to the show with Ginny and Carol and Charlotte, but Ginny had said to me, "I have a date."

"What do you mean, a date?"

"With a boy."

I hounded her for details. It turned out that Buddy Dolan had asked her if she was going to the show on Saturday afternoon. When Ginny said yes, he said, "See you there."

"That's a date?" I asked.

"Same thing, almost. If we all sit near the end of a row

and I'm on the end, he'll probably sit beside me."

"I thought we hated Buddy Dolan."

"We used to."

"Oh."

"Want to come?"

"I'd rather clean up my room." I was more than bitter. I scrutinized the situation as I kicked shoes into my closet and bunched up sweaters into balls and pitched them into open drawers. Buddy Dolan! What a bozo! If Ginny had to sit beside a boy, why couldn't she sit beside Patrick? He wouldn't mind, not now. I forced the dresser drawers shut on the sleeves and necks of sweaters. And then if Ginny had sat beside Patrick, I could have sat beside Alex, maybe. I tried to decide whether I really would have, and the decision was, yes. The worst had come to the worst. I liked a boy. And no birds were singing.

Ginny and Buddy Dolan! How could she? I made my bed, yanking the blankets up with such force that they came out at the foot. Patrick was ten times superior to Buddy Dolan. But when you thought about it, and I did think about it now, as I swished junk off my desk into the open drawer, Patrick, as he would be the first to admit, was limited. I hadn't paid attention to all that meant until now. Boys his age went to high-school dances. His former classmates would be driving cars in a year or so. Would Patrick ever be able to put his arms around a girl? Ginny would want all that as she got older. She would want car drives and dances and, well, everything, unless she could be persuaded that she *didn't* need all that. I seemed to have made a complete about-face in the jealousy department. Now I was throwing Ginny at Patrick.

I thought seriously about dragging my roller-skates back out of the trunk in the garage, but then I remembered the broken strap. Instead, I climbed the fence at the back of the house and went looking for the horses. I needed their company. They were waiting for me at the top of the high pasture. A brisk breeze lifted their manes and swept my hair behind me. I strode towards them on legs that felt as long and strong as a colt's. Here were my friends. They sauntered towards me, greeting me like one of their own.

Renewed, I watched from the front veranda as the boys returned later in the afternoon. John pushed the chair; Alex was talking, making wide gestures with his arms, far enough ahead of Patrick that he could see. They belted out laughter at whatever joke Alex had told. As they got closer I could see that Patrick was exhausted, but that something was shining behind his features that hadn't been there since before his polio. He looked animated.

They greeted me. With John on the back of the chair and Alex hoisting the front they had Patrick on the veranda without so much as a thump. John looked at his watch and said he had to get going. Patrick called something after him which meant nothing to me but did to them, and they all hooted with laughter. I remembered then that I had a hodge-podge of emotions, from resentment at being left out of today's outing to a possible crush on Alex. I opened the front door to go in.

Alex said, "Too bad you couldn't make it to the show, Keely."

I paused. "I couldn't?"

Patrick coughed slightly. His eyes slid away from mine.

"You would have liked it," Alex said.

"Probably." I looked steadily at Patrick but he wouldn't meet my gaze. I turned my attention again to Alex. I said, "The horses have all lost their marbles. Lola rolls in the grass like a dog and Bill has gone senile or something. He frisks around like a circus horse. Even Ginger acts like he has ants in his pants."

"It's spring," Alex explained. "They're feeling their oats. They could probably all use some exercise." He looked questioningly at me. "Sunday afternoon?"

"Well. . . ."

"Great! Hey, Patrick, come too. We'll harness up old Bill to the breadwagon. He's just itching to be back on the job."

"Don't know if I can. I'm kind of busy."

"Doing what?" I asked. "Inventing stories?"

Alex pushed Patrick's chair into the front hall. "See you tomorrow," he said, and closed the front door behind him.

I buttonholed Patrick with a glare. "And just what was the reason I couldn't go to the show?"

Patrick had the grace to look embarrassed. "I think I said you had to clean up your room or finish your homework or some such thing. I forget what I said. It was stupid. I should have talked to you first. I seem to do this lately, do stupid things first and regret them later. But I don't actually regret going without you."

"Thanks."

"I mean . . . boys are different when no girls are around. Ever since I've been sick I've been surrounded by women. It gets to you after a while. You just want to break loose from all the tender loving care." He looked carefully at me. I must have looked puzzled because he went on. "I'm not explaining it very well." He tried again. "With girls around, boys do things and say things to impress the girls. With no girls around . . . boys on their own push each other to the edge. There's always a risk you might look like a jerk, or not live up to some unexplained code. There's always a challenge. That's what I missed."

"We used to do that, you and I." I may have sounded wistful.

"What we did was a game. What I'm talking about is part of real life. I never used to think about it before; now I think about a lot of things. I had to go without you to test myself, to see if I had any . . . power."

Hesitantly I asked, "And do you?"

"Maybe. A little." He looked happy.

"Like what?"

"If I tried to explain it, it would sound like nothing. The thing that bugs me most, the thing that drove me to, almost to . . . it's helplessness. I can't physically help myself or anyone else. I'll always be the one who needs help. I'll never be the hero."

What could I say? I could invent lots of uplifting, phony expressions like, "You'll always be a hero to me," or, "You have a great mind." If I did, it would prove Patrick's point. If he had heard something like that a year ago he would have walked out of the room in disgust. Now he was powerless even to plug his ears. The situation seemed to call for something comforting and all I could think of was a toss-up between phoniness and silence. I looked glumly out from under my bangs and kept silent.

"Not a bad movie," he said, changing the subject.

"Did you see Ginny there?" I wheeled him into what was being turned into his new room, the former parlour.

"I don't know. I can't remember."

"Did Buddy Dolan sit beside her?"

"Probably." Patrick seemed to be interested in the view outside the window. Curtain material lay on the radiator under it.

"She should have sat beside you."

"She didn't see me. I was at the back on the other side." Patrick glanced at me. "What do you mean, she should have sat beside me? Why would she?"

"I just thought maybe you liked each other."

Patrick didn't say anything for a few minutes. "Don't muddle me up with other people, Keely. It won't work. Start seeing me the way I am. Okay? Sure I think Ginny's nice. I kind of like the way she didn't give up on me, just kept battering away. I couldn't even hurt her feelings. I hope she'll keep on being my friend. But as far as anything, you know, more serious goes, don't worry about me. I have a well-developed imagination, thanks to you and the dead soldier and . . . Ginny's letters."

"Ginny's letters?" I sat down on the radiator and tried to look like the kind of person a brother would want to confide in — innocent and not the least bit curious. It didn't work. He just looked back at me, secretive and a little bit smug. I knew hell would freeze over before I found out what was in those letters.

"I can make up daydreams," he went on, "and the great thing is, nobody knows who stars in them. Not even you!"

Sunday was as warm as a summer day. I jostled a reluctant Patrick up the lane to Sunny View Acres. "This is stupid," he said several times along the way. "You're all going to be riding horses and I'm going to be baking in the sun. I can't even twiddle my thumbs."

"You can ride in the breadwagon."

"I don't want to."

"What are you afraid of?"

"I'm not afraid of anything. It just doesn't sound like any fun."

We talked to the veterans for a few minutes, waiting for Alex to finish his chores. Charlotte came out of the house and joined us. "I got the invitation to your birthday, Keely. I'd just love to come."

"Swell."

"I'm getting a new dress. In Ottawa. Naturally."

"Natch."

"You can't get anything in Channing. What are you going to wear?"

I looked down at my khaki shorts that drooped a little too long, cast-offs of Patrick's, and the faded jersey stretched at the neck that completed my ensemble. "This, probably."

Charlotte rolled her eyes at Patrick. "Come and see what

Alex has done to that old breadwagon. He's been here since about six o'clock this morning working on it." I turned Patrick's chair towards the driveshed. Charlotte said, "Patrick wants me to push him, don't you, Patrick?" Before he was able to reply, Charlotte had taken over the back of his chair. Patrick turned his eyes to mine when I moved up beside him. He didn't have to say anything. His look meant: see what I mean about being helpless?

"I wouldn't mind horseback riding," she said, "if we had a small pony about this high." She indicated an animal slightly higher than a Labrador retriever. "Something I could control."

"You mean," said Patrick, "you don't want to abandon yourself to the whims of a large dumb animal."

I said, "Horses aren't so dumb."

"You know what I mean."

"I know what you mean," Charlotte piped up. "You and I are pretty much alike. We'd rather read books and stuff than go prancing around on a dumb horse."

"That's not what I meant," Patrick began. "I mean, I don't have any choice, do I? I can't ride. You can, if you choose. But if I could choose. . . ."

I guess this was over Charlotte's head. She interrupted, "Any time you want to borrow my Nancy Drews, I'll bring them over."

Patrick gave a small sigh. "I guess you're right, Charlotte. We're two of a kind. We both have our limitations."

Charlotte stopped pushing Patrick's chair suddenly, causing his head to bounce against the headrest. She sidled up to me and edged me a little away from Patrick. She whispered, "I used to think your brother was such a drip, but he's a lot nicer since he nearly died. I think he must be in love with me."

"You do?" I was startled.

"Boys fall in love with me all the time. Of course, I could

never fall in love with a cripple, but it won't kill me to be nice to him."

"You're all heart, Charlotte."

True to his word, Alex had revamped the breadwagon to accommodate Patrick. Old bits of harness had been nailed in place for safety straps, and a board padded with a small pillow would serve as a headrest. He had even managed to simulate Patrick's slings, using pieces of dowelling and strips torn from an old sheet.

"This looks as if it might work," I said. "Want us to lift you up there so you can try it out?"

"No."

"He's afraid," said Charlotte, "and I don't blame him."

"I'm not afraid. I'm waiting for Alex."

We hadn't long to wait. He soon came whistling into sight. Alex and Charlotte and I dragged the wagon out of the shed and pointed it towards the lane. Alex looked at Patrick. "Ready to test-drive this baby?"

Patrick contemplated the horseless carriage. "Sure, why not?" Alex took Patrick under the arms and stepped backwards up onto the running-board of the wagon. I had Patrick's legs and helped Alex swing him up onto the seat. Charlotte dithered back and forth saying, "Wait, you're dropping him," and "There must be an easier way." I gave her a look over my shoulder.

Once Patrick was safely strapped in, he grinned down at me. "Nothing to it. Safe as sitting in church."

Alex placed Patrick's arms in the slings. "We'll wrap the reins around your hands. That should work. It wouldn't take much of a pull to get Bill's attention. Laurence Saunders says he's been pulling this thing for more than ten years."

"Hey, wait a minute," said Patrick.

Alex interrupted. "Keely, all the horses are in the paddock. Bring Bill. Just snap the lead onto his halter. He'll come."

"Wait a minute!" Patrick called. I was on my way to the paddock and didn't stop. "I didn't think we were actually going to do this today," I heard Patrick yell.

"No time like the present," Alex said.

I was soon back, leading Bill. Alex had a mass of leather in his hands, sorting it out, preparing it for Bill. From the wagon bench, Patrick stared, pop-eyed, at the dumb animal I was attempting to position between the two shafts. I tried not to look at Patrick's startled eyes. "I see you have Lola all saddled up," I said to Alex. "I'd like to ride her."

"You better stick to Ginger. I'll ride Lola."

"I'm not afraid of her."

"She's unpredictable."

"Aren't we all? Look, trust me. I can manage her." I took off for the paddock again.

By the time Alex had Bill in harness and ready to pull the wagon, I was back on Lola, moving at a sedate walk. "See," I said, "I have her charmed. She loves me." Lola whinnied something to Bill. Bill ignored her. "I'll come along behind the breadwagon."

"We're not actually going anywhere, are we?" Patrick was beginning to break out into beads of sweat.

"If Patrick's afraid, then we shouldn't go," Charlotte said.

"I'm not afraid, exactly. It's just that we'll look stupid, like something that escaped from a circus."

Alex reassured him. "Nothing to worry about. I'll do the actual driving this time and we'll just go as far as the house and circle back. We're not going out on the road. I just want to see if it's *possible* for you to drive." Patrick's face didn't relax. "If," said Alex, "you want to."

"I'll come up beside you, Patrick." Charlotte had put on her mother-of-the-idiot voice, which was meant to soothe but only irritated. She climbed up beside Patrick and patted his arm. "There now."

"Let's try out my idea for these reins," Alex said. Bill

stood obediently between the shafts; he was used to waiting. Alex wound the reins around each of Patrick's wrists and looked critically at them. "I don't think that's going to work. They might not stay wound. I need some string or wire or something to fasten them to the slings. I'll be right back." He jumped down and went into the driveshed in search of materials.

Out on Fairly Street a car backfired. Lola bellowed and took off like something shot from a cannon. I bellowed too, and hung on for dear life. From a great distance I heard Patrick yell, "Come on, Bill, get up. Go after her!" Bill must have pricked up his ears like a colt, because I could hear him come thundering down the lane after his friend Lola. Alex told us sometime later that he had come out of the shed just in time to see our whole kit and caboodle take a right at Fairly and head out of town like bandits with a posse at our backs.

I managed to get my feet back in the stirrups, which gave me a little more stability, but pulling back on the reins had no effect on Lola. I slung myself low in the saddle and tried to move with the horse. If you can't beat 'em, I was thinking. . . . I managed a quick peek over my shoulder. The breadwagon was pitching along hard on my trail. Charlotte's mouth was a permanent O. Patrick's face had never looked more determined. I could hear him yell, "Whoa, Bill! Slow down!" Charlotte was yelling, "Somebody do something!"

The next time I looked back, the wagon was losing ground. Patrick seemed to have got Bill to slow down. I felt Lola ease up a bit, too. We had come to the marshy wooded area where the creek widens. Lola turned off the road and trotted in along a narrow path heading for Bloodsucker Pond, and I crouched low over her neck to avoid the tree branches. At the edge of the pond Lola stopped abruptly and lowered her head to drink. I didn't stop abruptly — I went right over her ears into the murky shallows.

I spluttered as I pulled my dripping, punished body from

the pond. I spat water from my mouth and shook it from my nose and ears. It dripped from my hair. When I had rubbed my eyes, I looked up into the two pale faces of Patrick and Charlotte in the breadwagon. Bill stood docilely in harness, pretending rescues were all in a day's work. "Keely, are you all right?" Patrick called.

"Am I all right?" I yelled back. "I fell head first into Bloodsucker Pond! How can I be all right?" I checked my arms for bloodsuckers.

"Don't worry." Patrick sounded reassuring. "It's too early for bloodsuckers."

I sighed with relief.

"Oh, yeah?" Charlotte piped up. "Then what's that black blob on her cheek?"

"Aargh!" I said. "Get it off me! Get it off me!" I ran up to Patrick and stood on the running-board of the wagon.

"I can't get it off you!"

"Charlotte," I yelled, "get it off!"

"I'm not touching that thing!" She shrank away.

I choked, "I'm going to throw up."

Calmly, Patrick said, "Take your fingernails and dig in around it and then pull. Then just chuck it away." I made blechy, throat-rasping sounds but followed Patrick's instructions. "There," said Patrick. "You can do anything if you put your mind to it."

"Holy!" I said. I stared in disbelief at him. Then I pointed at the horse and back to Patrick. "You actually came after me. Even though you — Patrick! I don't believe this!"

"What?"

"You actually came to rescue me."

"Well, somebody had to."

"He's not a very good driver," Charlotte grumbled. "He should have waited for Alex."

"Charlotte," I said, "why don't you shut your cute, dimpled face."

She humphed and put her nose in the air. "I'm telling," she said.

Alex arrived then, on Ginger. He looked relieved to see that we were all safe, but worry crept into his voice. "What are your parents going to say?" he asked Patrick. "They'll be mad at me. They'll never trust me again."

"They aren't going to know everything. Details can be so boring." Patrick grinned. I agreed with him.

"Well, anyway," said Alex, "we've got to get this circus act back to Sunny View somehow. We could tie the two horses to the back and I could drive, I guess."

"No problem," Patrick said. "I got us down here all right; I can get us back." Alex looked unsure but both Patrick and I insisted. We set off, Alex in the lead, the breadwagon next and me, all bedraggled, ambling behind on Lola. Our pace this time was funereal. "This is the stupidest thing we've ever done in our whole lives," Patrick said, loud enough for me to hear. I tried to think of something stupider but couldn't. "I never want to drive another horse as long as I live," he added.

"Why not," I yelled back, "now that you've got the hang of it?"

"You really want to know the truth?"

"What?"

"I'm scared stiff of horses. Always have been."

"Why didn't you say so?" Alex asked over his shoulder.

"Who knows?" Patrick muttered.

I knew.

At home that evening, we dwelt heavily on my gentle fall into Bloodsucker Pond. We touched ever so lightly on the fact that Patrick had had a little ride in the breadwagon. Our parents were horrified. "It was perfectly safe," Patrick insisted.

"I don't think risks like that are worth it," Father said. Patrick and I exchanged a Siamese glance.

Mother laid down the law. "I don't want you fooling around in that wagon any more."

Patrick smiled obligingly. "Okay."

"Funny," Peggy said. "It was a chariot, all right, but I thought it would be a longer trip, somehow — just from the configuration of the tea leaves."

Patrick and I looked thoughtfully at each other, our mouths hanging open just a little.

CHAPTER

14

"Look, if we get Peggy to tell us how to read tea leaves we can go around in the breadwagon and tell. . . ."

"No!"

"Everything she told you has come true. She must have learned it *somewhere*. No reason she can't teach us." We were in the former parlour, now Patrick's room. The sofa and chairs had been relocated to make room for Patrick's new bed, Peggy's rocker and my wicker chair. The room still had a faint smell of fresh paint.

"I'm not interested, Keely. I have more important projects at the moment." Patrick was trying to draw the head of a horse with his charcoal pencil. He was becoming exasperated. "It looks more like the head of a serpent," he complained.

"No, it's good."

"Keely, I don't need patronizing. I still have eyes in my head."

"I meant, for a serpent it's good." I was thinking again about Peggy and her fortune-telling gift. "All I want for my birthday is to have Peggy tell my fortune."

Patrick was working so hard that he was chewing on the side of his tongue. He had to put his head back, finally, to rest. "What if she sees something bad in it, the way she did in mine?"

"She didn't come right out and say something bad was

going to happen."

"I could tell by the look on her face," Patrick said.

"Nothing bad did happen to you."

"How can you say that?"

"You made something bad happen to yourself."

He looked at me with a degree of respect. "You've got a point."

"Maybe that's the whole idea," I went on, a little let down. "Maybe a fortune-teller doesn't really see into the future. Maybe she just tells you the possibilities. I mean, a wheelchair *would* be an obvious large surprise package for you, wouldn't it? And a trip? Well, nobody would go through life without taking a trip. She didn't specify when, or how long."

"Okay, how do you account for the chariot? Who'd have guessed that I'd take a trip in a breadwagon?"

I brightened. "Nobody. You're right. There is magic to it after all. I'm definitely going to ask her to read my teacup on my birthday."

My mother finally decided that a new dress was in order for the occasion of my thirteenth birthday. On Monday we walked downtown after school to look for something stylish. The stores in Channing had nothing chic except a black, imitation watered-silk, off-the-shoulder number which I thought was perfect. Mother thought differently. She took the train for Ottawa the next day to look for something in Ogilvy's or Murphy Gamble's to replace my old, too-short, red and green plaid with the Peter Pan collar. What she brought back was a longer plaid dress in subdued grey tones with an even sweeter collar and, of all things, a bow at the neck with long streamers trailing down the front. "It's very Junior Deb," she said. "Perfect for your party."

I ground my teeth.

My party lost some of its glamour when Linda Ford explained that she couldn't come because she hadn't been able to get out of going to her aunt's wedding. Then, when

Carol Katski's mother phoned to say Carol had the measles, I gave up. "Some friends they turned out to be!"

"You could invite Wendy and that nice girl Georgina," suggested Mother.

"They hate me."

"Oh, Keely."

"Well, they think I'm a screwball. Same thing. Anyway, it's too late now."

"Well, Charlotte's coming, and Ginny. You can always count on Ginny."

As it turned out, I couldn't. Friday, the day before my birthday, Ginny told me her bad news. "I know I should have told you before this," she said, "but every time I started to, I lost my nerve. I know what you're like." Apparently she had promised to babysit her little cousin the previous Saturday, but all memory of her commitment had disappeared with the prospect of her "date" with Buddy Dolan. "I just forgot to go babysitting, that's all. Jeepers, it's not my fault if I forgot. My mother acts as if it's the end of the world."

"What did she do?"

"She's making me stay in for the next four Saturdays."

I was stunned. "But my party!"

"Keel, I tried my best. I cried, I did everything. Look, I'll give you your present tonight."

"I don't want a present."

"I know what you mean." Ginny knew about Carol and Linda. Having already turned thirteen, she also understood what I had in store for me. A thirteenth birthday party with no guests, unless you wanted to count Charlotte! We both decided I might as well throw myself under a fast-moving train.

"Your mother might change her mind." But I wasn't hopeful.

Ginny just looked at me. We both knew Mrs. Dickson's word was law. "Somehow I'll make it up to you," Ginny said.

The sun shone on my birthday. I did my Saturday chores and didn't feel any older. I went over to Ginny's to see if she'd been granted parole. She hadn't. Mrs. Dickson, grim-faced, answered the door. "I'm sorry, Keely, but that child is going to learn to behave herself if she has to spend the rest of her life in her room." I trudged on home and thought, so this is my thirteenth birthday. A day like any other day, only more so. After lunch I turned on the radio. "Grand Central Station." I turned it off. I looked in on Patrick but he was asleep, or pretending to be asleep. He wasn't going to be very amusing in either case. By mid-afternoon I had begun to phi-losophize about birthdays. A birthday, I decided, is the one day in the whole year when you can depend on your friends to cheer for you, not for doing anything great, just for being there. At least, that's what other people's birthdays meant.

Late in the afternoon my mother called me into the kitchen, where she was beating up a batter of some sort. Cake, probably. I wasn't interested. "Why don't you go up and wash your hair and have a nice hot bath and put on your new grey dress."

"What's the point?"

"We're all getting dressed up, even Patrick."

"Aw, Mother. . . ."

"Hurry up now. By the time you're bathed and dressed your guests will be here."

"Guest," I reminded her with distaste.

"Never mind, Charlotte will be just fine. You can open your presents in the living-room and then we'll have all your favourite things for dinner."

"Ketchup sandwiches?" I knew instantly from her expres-sion that ketchup sandwiches would not be on the menu. "Do I actually have to take a bath?"

"Just to please me."

I groaned but climbed the stairs. Peggy came out of the bathroom on a cloud of scented steam. "Going to get cleaned up, Keely?"

"Why bother?"

"It's your birthday."

"So why should I be a big phony just because it's my birthday?"

"You're the only person I've ever met who thinks being clean is phony."

"You have to admit it isn't natural."

Peggy shook her head. She went into her room to slip into something soft and flowery, she said, in honour of my birthday.

I had nothing better to do. I headed for the bathroom and turned on both taps full blast. Afterwards, examining my gleaming face in the mirror, I had a flash of insight. Just like that. I could see now that I had been pursuing the wrong path all my life. I shouldn't have been trying to be a hero. Heroes are screwballs. I should have been trying to be a real person like everyone else. Real people like to keep clean and wear neat, fashionable clothes. Also, their faces look right. The real people of this world, the ones whose friends show up for their birthdays, the ones who have boys falling all over them (not while accidentally catching a baseball), these people have a certain look about them. Some even have dimples.

I poked the end of my comb into my cheeks but the effect was short-lived and painful. I re-examined my face and noted the lack of kiss curls. I twisted my bangs into coils and tried to secure them with bobby-pins. Smooth people manage this without effort. Not me. I gave up, but not before I'd found a way around the problem. If I took my comb and wound my bangs around it and then rolled the comb right up tight to my forehead and left it until my hair dried, I'd get a big, beautiful curl. That would be a start. I was beginning to feel like a member of the human race, even though I looked peculiar with a comb pressed to my forehead and an angry red spot on each cheek.

Eyebrows were next on my critical list. I was the only girl

in Channing, in the entire Ottawa Valley, maybe in the whole of Ontario, whose eyebrows were so thick that, if they continued to grow, they'd blind me. Not only that, they appeared to be trying to join over my nose in one straight, furry line, which made me look like a gorilla. Real people — models, movie stars and the like — had pencil-thin, arched eyebrows that made them look genteel, although maybe a little startled.

I'd remedy the situation with my father's razor. I began with the centre bit above the bridge of my nose. It wasn't all that easy. However, I whittled and scraped away until I'd removed a good-sized hairy section at about centre face, creeping perhaps a little too far to the left. To balance this, I sliced a generous path through my right eyebrow — a little too generous. I was beginning to look quizzical. I'd never really noticed before how my eyebrows were attempting to obliterate my entire face. They grew up towards my hairline, out towards my ears, and even underneath they seemed to be reaching down to get friendly with my eyelids. The top part was easy: I just rasped over those unwanted hairs until what remained was a very thin line, left and right. Not bad. The underneath part was the killer. My skin was very tender there and I had to start up pretty high to get at those stubborn, unsightly eyebrow-hairs — so high, in fact, that I lost my thin line entirely. I was left with a skimpy section of eyebrow far to the left side of my face, and not so much as a bristle on the right. I no longer looked like a gorilla; I looked like the brainless wonder of the world. A cold, panicky feeling overwhelmed me. I'd obviously gone about as far as I could go.

"Keely, what's the hold-up?" My family was waiting for me.

"Coming," I called back, hoarsely and not very loudly. My hair was half dry. By the time I got dressed it would be dry enough for me to unroll the comb. Perhaps Mother wouldn't notice my eyebrows, or rather lack of them, entranced as she would be by the sausage roll of curls across my forehead.

I took time dressing. At least I had the comfort of knowing that my dress was very Junior Deb — an important factor if you've decided to become a real person like everyone else.

"Come down and open your presents, Keely!"

"In a minute," I called back. I still had my hair to do. I went back into the bathroom and nearly died of shock when I caught a fresh peek at my bald face. "Ohmygosh," I whispered. I began to unroll the comb. Or at least I began to try. The comb was stuck. Thoroughly stuck. I tugged at a few strands of hair, hoping to free my forehead from the comb that way, but it was too painful. My bangs were too long. They were securely rolled up. For ever.

The cold, panicky, disappearing-eyebrow feeling was replaced by a hot, sweaty, how-can-I-live-with-a-comb-stuck-to-my-forehead feeling.

"Dinner will be ruined if you don't get down here for your presents, Keely."

"I'll be right there!" I called, my voice a little high-pitched. I opened the top drawer of the bathroom dresser, took out Mother's nail scissors and cut the comb out of my hair. The short, toothbrush-like row across the front of my head didn't do a thing for me. If it had been someone else's blank face looking back, I might have had a good hoot. But it was my own, Keely the Connor, hero of lesser causes, seeker after outer beauty. I wrapped myself in an imaginary cloak of dignity and descended.

"Keely, is that you?" called my mother from the kitchen as I reached the hall below.

"Yes."

"Go into the living-room and turn on the lights. We'll be there in a minute."

The living-room drapes were always closed in the evening. Without a murmur I did as I was asked. A lamp stood on a table just inside the door. I would turn on only that and then retreat to the far end of the room. From that distance my defects might not bowl my family over at first glance. I pulled the little brass chain on the lamp, turned from the sudden brightness and gaped.

"HAPPY BIRTHDAY!" they yelled.

"Holy *toot!*" I said.

Patrick, my father, Peggy and Charlotte were no surprise. Alex was. His ears stuck out only a little bit because he was smiling. It turned out Patrick had invited him, and he seemed glad to be there. Charlotte, on the other hand, was not smiling. Smart as paint in a duplicate of my Junior Deb, she looked like a thundercloud. Mother stood in the doorway. It was very exciting, very noisy, then suddenly very quiet.

"Keely! what on earth have you done to your eyebrows?" Mother sounded shrill.

As nonchalantly as possible, I said, "Shaved them off."

"And your bangs! Keely!"

"Cut 'em."

There were gasps. There were more questions. A giggle. Outright laughter. I stood tall and straight and took it. What else could I do? I felt a bit like Joan of Arc explaining her voices.

Patrick didn't laugh. He studied me silently, seriously. For once, I couldn't read his mind. We were definitely two separate people. Peggy said that she thought she could fix me up with eyebrow pencil and that maybe the bristle-bangs effect would catch on at school and start a fad. Charlotte, still suffering the shock of seeing me, Keely Connor, in *her* dress, fetched all the way from Ottawa especially for the occasion, said she doubted that it would, that it wouldn't have in Ottawa, that's for sure.

I opened my presents and was properly appreciative, although quiet. I felt naked, exposed, without a hedge of bangs to peep out from under, and curiously bland without eyebrows to show the world my feelings. There is such a thing, I thought, as being a fraction too real. I yearned for my old screwball-hero identity.

"Dinner will be on the table in five minutes," Mother announced, heading for the kitchen. Peggy and Father went out to help, leaving me, Charlotte and Alex to escort Patrick into the dining-room.

"Wait a sec," Alex said. "I have a present for you too." I was surprised, although I don't suppose my face showed it. He handed me a small wrapped box to open. Inside was a charm bracelet with a single charm — a horse pulling a carriage. "I could have got a horse only, but it seemed too ordinary. I thought you'd like this as a . . . symbol, if that's the right word."

"What does that mean?" Charlotte asked.

Patrick and I exchanged a quick glance, the shadow of a grin on our faces. Patrick said, "It's what they clash together at the end of a drum roll."

"Oh." Charlotte looked vague.

I didn't need eyebrows to show Alex my delight. I must have looked as though I might throw my arms around him and give him a big kiss. He looked guardedly at me, his head tilted away a little, as if he was afraid I might — but not too far, as if he was hoping I would.

Charlotte asked for a closer look at the charm bracelet. She examined it under the light and called Alex over to ask him if it was real silver. Patrick chose the moment to say quietly to me, "You look like nobody on earth."

"You said it." I looked glumly at the floor.

"You look like one of those saints, like somebody in a painting. Or somebody who should be in a painting."

I looked up. Was this a compliment? Was this Patrick? Was this the sort of thing real people heard said to them every day? "I thought I looked like a goofball," I said.

"Only a little bit," he assured me.

After dinner, Peggy didn't have to be coaxed to read my teacup. The ritual was just getting under way when we heard a light tapping at the kitchen door. I said I'd see what it was, and left everyone in the dining-room, straining their ears. All they heard, probably, was my muffled squeal of surprise and Ginny's strangled shriek of laughter. Every time she looked at my face she exploded. When she could talk she said, "You're supposed to *pluck* them, moron," and then collapsed again. I knew it was funny, but was it that funny? I urged her to come into the dining-room.

"Your parents will *die*!"

I dragged a shame-faced Ginny behind me. "But, Ginny. . . ," my mother began.

"I sneaked out through the cellar window. She doesn't know I'm gone," Ginny blurted, as if expecting to be reprimanded by the parental figures. Father gave every indication of beginning a "law and order" lecture, but merely harrumphed after he got a gentle "quality of mercy is not strained" look from Mother. "I just had to," Ginny continued. "After all, when your best friend turns thirteen you get desperate, don't you?" Coming from Ginny, this sounded logical. "Here's your present, Keely." She thrust a small gift into my hand. Inside was a tube of luscious, dark, cherry-coloured lipstick.

"Oh Ginny, thank you!" I clasped it tight and closed my eyes. "This is the ultimate. Katharine Hepburn would give her life for it."

"Isn't she a bit young?" Father asked quietly.

"Yes dear," said Mother, "but it's having it that counts."

"I see," he said, and looked puzzled. Patrick didn't look at all puzzled.

Ginny greeted the others. I had the brief, uncharitable feeling that her smile for Alex was a trifle too bright.

"G'day, Patrick," Ginny said jauntily. Patrick returned her greeting and I noticed a faint flow of colour creeping from his neck into his cheeks.

"So what's new, Ginny?" Patrick sounded offhand.

"Not much."

Father placed a chair beside Patrick for her. Ginny thanked him and sat down.

Trying not to sound embarrassed, Patrick said, "Why don't you come over sometime and I'll teach you how to play chess?" I noticed that he had worked both arms out of his slings. They lay folded on his tray as natural as anything.

"Could I?" Ginny's voice betrayed her astonishment at the change in Patrick. "I'd love to. And I already know how to play chess." Patrick's face dropped slightly. Ginny quickly continued, "But not very well. I need to brush up." If there was one thing Ginny understood, it was boys.

"You're on."

"As soon as I get out of jail."

Mother was becoming nervous. Rules were, after all, as she often pointed out, rules. She said, "I hate to be a spoilsport, but. . . ."

"I know," said Ginny. "Back to my ball and chain." She waved a half-salute to Patrick. To her amazement, slowly and shakily he returned the gesture. Ginny beamed at him as if he had just turned a double cartwheel for her benefit.

"Try and stay out of trouble, kiddo," he said, and winked. Ginny dashed.

The reading of the birthday teacup once again took precedence. Peggy was the focus of attention. She turned my inverted cup three times in its saucer and then slowly, tantalizingly righted it. She peered into it at arm's length. She scrutinized it at close quarters. She snorted. She looked heavenward and shook her head in disbelief.

"Come on, Peggy." I was dying of curiosity.

"This is amazing! Look!" Peggy displayed it all around the table. "Everything points to hugeness. The grand scale."

"What does it mean?"

"It means no half-measures for you, Keely. Whatever you do, you'll do with a bang."

"Will I go on a trip?"

"Trip?" Peggy studied the teacup. "I'd say you'll see half the world."

"Will I be happy?"

"Ecstatic."

"Won't I ever be sad?"

Peggy paused. She nodded. "Unbearably," she said quietly.

"But not for ever, I hope."

"Goodness, no. Look at this. It's almost like a coiled spring. Nothing can keep you down. Nothing can hold you back. And look at this. You don't often see this so clearly." She pointed out two circles of tea leaves.

"What does it mean?"

"Completion," Peggy said. "Plans work out. Something like that." She looked at me. I studied the cup and nodded my head knowingly. I had my elbows on the table now, and was leaning my chin on my hands staring at Peggy in amazement. I was sorry when she put the cup down.

"My turn," I said quickly and took *her* cup before she could protest. I did everything right, turned it three times, peered into it, squinted my eyes and tried to look as mysterious as possible.

"Well," Peggy said, one eyebrow raised, "what do you see?"

What I saw mostly looked like tea leaves. I tried to think symbolically. Through half-closed eyes, and with my head tilted, I saw something. "What you have here is more than a circle," I said. "This is a ring, an actual ring." When I looked at her, Peggy looked quite pink. "It's like an engagement ring. That's what it means, doesn't it? Marriage."

Peggy scoffed, "No one believes that kind of nonsense any more." But she was still pink when she said it. She reached for the cup, but I leaned back and looked closer even though nothing else stood out as clearly as the ring. We were all kind of quiet, thinking, I guess, about its significance.

Charlotte looked around the table at all the serious faces. She shrank into herself a little, as if frightened. "This gives me the willies. It's all just made up, you know. Nobody can really tell fortunes." Her voiced seemed too loud.

I ignored her and passed *my* cup back to Peggy. "Anything there about horses?"

Peggy twisted my cup and squinted at it with one eye. "Herds of them," she said. "Look at that. Galloping across the bottom and right up the other side."

After the teacup reading, the party broke up. Alex said he had to leave. Charlotte leaned close to my ear and said, "I'd better get going too. Alex probably wants to walk me home." He was nearly out the door. "Wait, Alex," she called, "I'm coming." I thought I saw his shoulders sag a little.

Nothing was left of the party but the dishes. By rights I shouldn't have had to do them, not on my birthday, but I was thirteen and quite mature. Father went into the living-room to read the paper and Peggy and I cleared the table. Patrick offered to come into the kitchen to supervise. I dragged a dishtowel across a plate and stuck it in the cup-board. "We don't need supervision," I told him.

"You do so. Look! That plate's still wet on the bottom."

I threw my dishtowel at him. It bounced off his head and landed on the floor.

"More company," Peggy predicted.

"Not at this hour, I hope." Mother glanced up at the clock.

"Maybe Ginny'll make another escape." I figured she was capable of it.

Mother was down to washing the last pot. Peggy took my dishtowel and said she'd finish drying, and I didn't object at all. I wheeled Patrick out of the kitchen and into his new room.

"I've got something I want to show you," he said. "Get

around in front of me."

I got around in front of his wheelchair and just then we heard the telephone ringing in the front hall. I started to go for it, but he said, "Wait! You've got to see this." So I went back. We heard Father answer it. "Watch my knee," Patrick said.

I stared at his bony knees in the new flannel trousers Mother had finally had to get him. "Which one?"

"The right."

"Peggy!" we heard Father call. "A gentleman would like to speak to you on the telephone."

I stopped looking at Patrick's knee and looked into his face. He looked into mine too, and I knew what he was thinking. "The dead soldier," I said.

Patrick shook his head. "Uh-uh. It's Laurence Saunders. Keep in mind this is real life, Keel."

"I know that. That's why I'm sure it's Peggy's soldier. Why don't I just accidentally walk past the telephone?"

"Because you're supposed to be looking at something I want to show you. Concentrate on my right knee."

I concentrated on Patrick's right knee. It quivered, then slowly, magically, it came up high enough to bump the bottom of his tray. His leg went back down with a thump and he sat there panting, catching his breath. In his eyes was a look of triumph.

Peggy's romance, at that moment, took a decided back seat in my life. I wanted to jump up and down and yell hurray at the top of my lungs and throw my arms around Patrick's neck and hug him to pieces, but I knew he'd only tell me to get away. So I grinned. More than grinned. I probably beamed. "You're going to do all right," I said. "You're going to survive."

He actually beamed back. "I have so far." His voice, when he said that, sounded powerful.

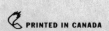

PRINTED IN CANADA